# Di

*Divine Cozy Mystery Series*

## Book 1

# Hope Callaghan

**hopecallaghan.com**
Copyright © 2019
All rights reserved.

***** *****

This book is a work of fiction. Although places mentioned may be real, the characters, names and incidents, and all other details are products of the author's imagination and are fictitious. Any resemblance to actual organizations, events, or actual persons, living or dead is purely coincidental.

No part of this publication may be copied, reproduced in any format, by any means, electronic or otherwise, without prior consent from the copyright owner and publisher of this book.

---

**Visit my website for new releases and special offers:  hopecallaghan.com**

i

# Acknowledgements

Thank you to these wonderful ladies who help make my books shine - Peggy H., Cindi G., Jean P., Wanda D., Barbara W. and Renate P. for taking the time to preview *Divine Intervention,* for the extra sets of eyes and for catching all of my mistakes.

**A special THANKS to my reader review teams, here in the U.S., and those across the pond, over the border and an ocean away!**

Alice, Amary, Barbara, Becky, Brinda, Cassie, Charlene, Christina, Debbie, Dee, Denota, Devan, Grace, Jan, Jo-Ann, Joyce, Jean K., Jean M., Katherine, Lynne, Megan, Melda, Kat, Linda, Lynne, Pat, Patsy, Paula, Rebecca, Rita, Tamara, Valerie, Vicki and Virginia.

Allie, Anca, Angela, Ann, Anne, Bev, Bobbi, Bonny, Carol, Carmen, David, Debbie, Diana, Elaine, Elizabeth, Gareth, Ingrid, Jane, Jayne, Jean, Joan, Karen, Kate, Kathy, Lesley, Margaret, Marlene, Patricia, Pauline, Sharon, Sheila and Susan.

# CONTENTS

ACKNOWLEDGEMENTS ...........................................II
PROLOGUE.................................................................1
CHAPTER 1 ................................................. 5
CHAPTER 2.................................................21
CHAPTER 3.................................................. 35
CHAPTER 4................................................. 49
CHAPTER 5................................................. 62
CHAPTER 6.................................................75
CHAPTER 7.................................................91
CHAPTER 8................................................. 108
CHAPTER 9................................................. 121
CHAPTER 10 .................................................134
CHAPTER 11................................................. 151
CHAPTER 12 .................................................173
CHAPTER 13 .................................................192
CHAPTER 14 ................................................. 207
CHAPTER 15 ................................................. 226
CHAPTER 16 ................................................. 238
CHAPTER 17................................................. 255
CHAPTER 18 .................................................261
CHAPTER 19 ................................................. 271
CHAPTER 20.................................................285
GET FREE EBOOKS AND MORE..........................291
LIST OF HOPE CALLAGHAN BOOKS .............. 292
MEET THE AUTHOR ................................... 297
CHOCOLATE CHIP, BANANA NUT MUFFINS
RECIPE....................................................... 299

# Prologue

Raylene Baxter crawled on top of the metal railing. She swung her legs over the side of the bridge and shot a quick glance at the road behind her.

The coast was clear...not a vehicle in sight, giving Raylene a few moments to contemplate her past forty plus years of bad decisions.

The last several had been the worst. Languishing in a women's prison for the last decade had also given her plenty of time to reflect on what went wrong.

She absentmindedly brushed a pile of pebbles off the railing, watching them drop into the ravine and the water below. One of them landed in her sandal and wedged between her toes. Raylene pressed down, forcing the small pebble to dig into the tender flesh on the side of her toes.

The hum of tires on the hot pavement caught her attention. She shaded her eyes and watched as a car approached. The driver slowed before picking up speed. The car crested the hill and disappeared from sight.

Raylene reached into the front pocket of her tattered jeans, the pair she'd been wearing the day she was arrested, and pulled out the debit card the parole officer handed her yesterday, the day she was released from prison.

She was a free woman, but not really. Raylene was a prisoner of her past. She turned the card over in her hand, contemplating leaving it behind for someone else. She wouldn't need it - not where she was going.

Her thoughts drifted to her close friend, Brock, as they did every single day for the past decade.

Raylene's rap sheet included being an accomplice to murder...her friend Brock's murder. She hadn't pulled the trigger of the gun that took his life, although her court-appointed attorney failed to convince the jury of that fact.

But she might as well have. This was one more failure Raylene added to her long list of failures. The failures rolled through her mind like a never-ending list of movie credits. Bad decisions, bad luck and just plain bad company.

For once in her life, she was going to do something right.

Raylene flicked the debit card in the air and watched it spin before going down...down until it turned into a tiny speck and disappeared from sight.

She removed her left shoe. The shoe followed the debit card. Her right shoe was next.

"This is it." Raylene slowly stood, her legs trembling as she shifted back ever so slightly. Soon, it would all be over. Raylene Baxter's miserable, pathetic life had reached an inevitable end.

She sucked in a shaky breath, sudden tears welling up in her eyes. Raylene slowly lifted her gaze skyward. "God, if you're out there. If you do exist, I'm sorry."

Before Raylene could change her mind, she leaped off the edge, letting out a small gasp as her trembling body hurtled at breakneck speed toward the ravine, the dark, deep waters and her death.

# Chapter 1

"This will simply not do." Joanna Pepperdine placed her hands on her slim hips, studying the labels on the jars of honey. Nash Greyson, her handyman, didn't slow as he continued arranging them in a neat row.

"Now what's wrong with them, Jo? I put them right where you wanted, front and center." Nash motioned to the entrance of *Second Chance Mercantile*. "Business is brisk today. Who cares if the labels are peeling off? These jars of pure honey will be gone before you hang the *Closed* sign by the end of today."

"It's all about quality and presentation." Jo grabbed a jar and finished peeling the label off. "Customers want a good deal. They also want to know they're purchasing a quality product. If they see our labels peeling off, they'll start questioning the quality of the honey."

A shopper carrying a basket brimming with baked goods approached the table. "Good afternoon, Jo. I see your honey is finally out. I'll take two." The woman promptly placed two jars of honey next to a box of red velvet cookies. "I see the label is peeling off. Would you consider giving me a ten percent discount for damaged goods?"

Jo snatched the jars of honey from the woman's basket. "I will not. The labels are a little loose, but you're getting some top-notch honey, fresh as of this morning. I can sell that honey all day long at full price."

"I meant no harm." The woman reached for the jar. "I still want the honey. Are you all right? You seem a little uptight."

Jo's expression softened. "I'm sorry, Marlee. I didn't mean to snap at you. It's been a long day."

Marlee Davison, Jo's friend and the owner of *Divine Delicatessen*, smiled. "Is someone else giving you a hard time?"

"You could say that. The Smith County Chamber of Commerce sent me a notice. They received an anonymous tip that I'm operating an unlicensed bed and breakfast, so they're sending someone out to investigate."

"It's probably that evil Debbie Holcomb again. I wish that woman would leave you alone," Marlee said. "Maybe if you invited her for tea and a tour of the farm, she would change her mind about your home and businesses."

Jo tugged on a strand of her silvery-blond hair. "I don't think it will help."

"I disagree. I think you need to make more of an effort to get to know your neighbors. Why don't you come by my delicatessen for a meal? It is the local's hangout. While you're there, you can have a look around, maybe stop by some of the other businesses and introduce yourself."

"We'll see," Jo said noncommittally. "I stay pretty busy."

Marlee straightened her back. "There are some nice folks in Divine, some decent people. Of course, there are also a few stinkers like Debbie Holcomb. I think it would do you and the women a world of good if you got to know some of the locals."

The farm was much more than a second chance for some of the current female residents. For some, it was the last chance. Not only was Jo's mercantile and baked goods store part of her farm, but it was also home to a half dozen women, down on their luck with nowhere to go.

The female residents were all recent releases from the *Central State Women's Penitentiary*. The penitentiary was in the middle of nowhere; a place most residents of Northern Kansas never even knew existed. It was in the same county as their small town of Divine, but still miles away.

The town of Divine, population 1,216 according to the most recent census, was mostly retired folks.

Despite the remote location, there was a steady stream of people passing through.

Divine was near the geographic center of the contiguous United States. There wasn't much to see at the local landmark, just a couple of signs, a small church and farm fields for as far as the eye could see.

Jo had visited once. She took a quick look around and then hopped back in her car. She had no idea what attracted the tourists and curiosity seekers, but as she liked to say, "Never look a gift horse in the mouth." And as long as they came, they stopped by her place to shop at the mercantile, buy baked goods from her bakeshop and purchase Jo's organic fruits and vegetables.

One of Jo's current "house guests" traipsed inside the store, to relieve Jo and not a moment too soon.

Her feet had been giving her a touch of trouble lately, but Jo refused to let it slow her down. There were people depending on her.

"It's been a busy one, Kelli. Did you finish helping Delta with the last of the banana nut loaves?"

"Yes, ma'am." Kelli's head bobbed up and down. "She was whipping up a batch of fried chicken for dinner when I left."

Jo patted her stomach. "Delta makes the best fried chicken."

Delta was Jo's second-in-command, chief cook and head "housemother" when Jo wasn't around. Truth be told, Jo was certain if Delta hadn't joined her, she wouldn't be able to keep the doors open and house the female residents.

God had blessed Jo Pepperdine, giving her exactly what she needed when she needed it.

"My feet are giving me fits today." Jo thanked Marlee for the offer and promised to try to stop by her restaurant the following day.

She limped across the gravel drive, slowly making her way up the steps of her stately Victorian. She made it as far as the door where she found her old hound, Duke, sprawled out in front of the porch swing.

Jo greeted her faithful pup before easing onto the swing, a painful sigh escaping her lips.

Duke flopped over so that he was directly under Jo's feet. She kicked her shoes off and lightly placed her feet on his furry side. "Duke, what are we gonna do about my aching feet?"

She shifted her gaze to the road watching the cars that pulled in and out of the parking lot. Moments later, a familiar four-door sedan pulled onto the gravel drive.

Instead of driving toward the mercantile, the car turned, heading along the circular drive to the house. It stopped near the front steps.

Duke opened one eye and promptly closed it again.

"Some guard dog you are." Jo watched Pastor Sawyer Murphy ease out of his car and make his way up the steps.

"Pastor Murphy." Jo wiggled to a sitting position. "Delta called to let you know the honey is finally ready?"

"She may have." The pastor absentmindedly tapped his pocket. "I've been out all day making my rounds and haven't had time to listen to my messages."

"We set aside a couple of jars. They're in the kitchen. Delta is guarding them like a hawk."

The pastor smiled. "I've been thinking about that honey ever since you told me there was some coming in, although that's not why I'm here."

Jo patted the empty seat next to her. "Have a seat. Duke and I were resting for a spell."

"Thanks." The pastor climbed the steps and removed his hat. "This one's a scorcher."

"That it is," Jo agreed. "We could use some rain to cool things off. If you're not here to pick up the honey, I take it you're here to talk shop."

"I am." Sawyer ran his finger along the rim of his hat. "I thought I would stop by to see if you have any open spots. If I recall correctly, the last time I dropped by you told me you had a full house."

"I did. Emily, one of the gals, is leaving tomorrow morning. She has family down in Oklahoma City driving up to get her."

"That's good news. Emily is a sweet woman." The pastor cleared his throat. "I have somewhat of a unique situation for you this time."

Jo lifted a brow. "Aren't they all unique? I mean, all of the women you send over here."

Pastor Murphy and Jo became friends not long after Jo arrived in Divine and she purchased the auctioned property, a Victorian home, and some outbuildings.

The property, described as a turn-of-the-century Victorian with ten acres of land, with potential for income properties, was up for auction. It was as if God had dropped it in her lap.

The pastor stopped by one day, curious about the newcomer and having heard the rumors circulating around town about the single woman who was fixing up the old McDougall place.

When Jo told him her plans for the property, the pastor recommended Nash, a Divine resident and skilled handyman. He arranged a meeting between the two, and Jo hired him on the spot.

Nash had been instrumental in implementing Jo's plans. They spent weeks tackling some much-needed repairs to the main house and guest quarters.

Since purchasing the home and properties, the team of two worked tirelessly, fixing up the pole building, sandwiched between the main house and the guest quarters.

He had been a blessing from above and helped Jo turn her vision into reality. Nash not only helped Jo create a haven for homeless women, but also sources of income.

Upon completion of the repairs to the pole barn, *Divine Baked Goods Shop* and *Second Chance Mercantile* were born.

During the pastor's second visit to check on Jo's progress, he confessed that some of the Divine residents were less than thrilled about Jo's arrival.

The pastor was blunt, warning her that although the residents of Divine were good people, they didn't take kindly to newcomers. Finally, he admitted it was because of the nearby women's prison, and he flat out asked Jo if she came from the prison.

Instead of answering him, she posed a question of her own...What woman released from a women's correctional facility could afford to purchase one of the largest pieces of property in the area?

She also told him he could take that answer right back to town. Pastor Murphy never brought it up again, and neither did Jo. The truth was Jo was very familiar with the women's prison, but not in a way most might suspect.

For days after the pastor's visit, Jo mulled over his confession and the area residents' concerns. If the town folks were concerned about Jo's past, wait until they discovered her reason for purchasing the property.

Despite her concerns, Jo pressed on with her plans for not only opening the mercantile and baked goods shop but also turning her home into a halfway house for former female convicts, to give them what they desperately needed - a second chance.

"Have you found someone to fill the empty spot?" Jo asked.

"Maybe," Pastor Murphy said. "Evan, one of the locals, helped rescue a woman the other day. She jumped off the *Divine Bridge*."

Jo clasped a hand to her chest. "She jumped off the bridge and lived?"

"Believe it or not, yes. Evan was passing by on his way to work. He saw the woman sitting on the railing. Something about her made him think she might be in trouble. He turned around to go back to talk to her, but it was too late."

"Evan saw her go over," Jo whispered.

"Yes. When he got to the railing and looked over the side to see where she went, he spied two men pulling the woman out of the water. By the time he reached the riverbank, the men were gone."

"Another divine intervention?" Marlee, the deli owner, told her the stories of miraculous rescues, unexplained near misses and mysterious figures with glowing faces, towering over them and rescuing residents in peril.

In fact, Jo had encountered one such angelic being, right after purchasing the property. Nash and she had spent the day replacing some of the outlets in the house, including several that weren't working.

It was a long day, but Nash and she finally completed the task. An exhausted Jo fell into bed and into a deep sleep that night.

During the night, someone rolled her to the edge of the bed, abruptly awakening her. Frightened, Jo flung the covers off, certain that someone had snuck into her bedroom and planned to attack her.

Duke, who was sleeping on the floor near the door, began growling and ran out of the bedroom.

Jo grabbed her robe and started to follow him when she realized the room smelled of electrical burning. She turned on her bedside lamp and discovered that one of the outlets was smoking. Jo ran downstairs and quickly flipped the breaker off.

She rushed upstairs to put the fire out and then woke Nash, who was asleep in his small apartment above the mercantile.

Jo promptly called an electrician early the next morning. When he arrived, he told them that they'd accidentally crossed some wires, causing them to spark. The electrician fixed the problem and checked the rest of the wiring before he left.

After the close call, Nash and Jo both agreed they would no longer tackle projects that involved electricity and instead, would hire a professional.

With no explanation of who pushed Jo, causing her to wake, she wondered if perhaps she'd had an angelic encounter.

Duke refused to step foot inside the bedroom for several days despite her coaxing. She decided to do some online research and found that the pets of people who claimed they had an angelic encounter were terrified to go near the area where the visitation occurred.

Since then, she'd discovered others in the small town reported visits as well.

"What's her story?" Jo asked.

"She's being released from the hospital tomorrow. Her name is Raylene Baxter. I caught a glimpse of her driver's license on the tray next to her hospital bed. The license is expired and lists an address in another state."

"Expired." Jo studied the pastor thoughtfully. "She's probably from the prison."

The pastor nodded. "She told the doctor she has nowhere to go. No family. No friends."

"She's in a dark place." Jo's throat clogged. Another lost soul with nowhere to go... She knew all about dark places, having been in one for a very long time herself.

"So? Will you consider taking Raylene in?"

# Chapter 2

"What's her story? Why was she in prison?"

Pastor Murphy shifted uncomfortably. "Raylene was convicted of being an accomplice to a crime." He hurried on. "It was the murder of her friend and business partner. She swears she wasn't the one who killed him."

Jo's rules for the residents were strict. One of those rules was that the women living there had not been convicted of murder. She was adamant about the rule, number one on her list.

"I believe everyone deserves a second chance, but for the safety of the women here, not to mention that of my staff and myself, you know I don't allow convicted killers," Jo said. "Now if her conviction involved drugs, robbery or fraud, it would be a different story."

Even then, Jo was careful to screen the women with background checks and online resources; she also interviewed each of them extensively. There was no sense in wasting their time or hers if they planned to return to a life of crime.

Because of this, Jo turned away a few, for various reasons.

"But Raylene is different," the pastor argued. "I've done some digging around myself. She was at the scene of her friend's death and was even able to identify the person who pulled the trigger. I'm almost certain she did not kill the man."

Jo shook her head while Murphy pressed on. "Will you at least talk to her? I think you might have a change of heart."

Another of Jo's requirements was the women were committed one hundred percent to starting over, to learn new skills to support themselves, and promised never to return to the way of life that got them in trouble in the first place.

The fact that Raylene attempted suicide was of particular concern to Jo. The last thing she needed was for the woman to finish what she started and for one of the other women, in a fragile frame of mind themselves, to find her body.

"I believe she would jump at the chance. It seems her near-death experience had a profound effect on her. She said that right before she jumped off the side of the bridge, she told God she was sorry."

A chill ran down Jo's spine. The fact that Evan, the man who found Raylene, spotted two large men, who disappeared by the time he reached the woman, was a sign of an angelic encounter. The fall should've mangled the woman's body.

"Well..." Jo studied the pastor thoughtfully. "I suppose it wouldn't hurt. You said you're going to pick her up in the morning?"

"Yes." The pastor settled his hat atop his head and stood. "I'll pick her up, take her out for breakfast and then stop by the mercantile to purchase some clothes. While we're here, you can chat with Raylene, and then decide whether you want to tell her about this place."

Jo followed his lead and slowly rose to her feet. "What happens to Raylene if I don't take her in?" Although she asked the question, she was sure she already knew the answer and so did Pastor Murphy.

"Like I said, she has nowhere to go. There's a chance she'll head back to the bridge and finish what she started. She could also take off for the city and end up living on the streets. You know the statistics as well as I do, Jo." The pastor stepped over to the stairs, his gaze drawn to *Second Chance Mercantile's* bustling parking lot.

"God has His hand on you, Jo. I'm not sure why He chose Divine, Kansas. Only He could create a successful business in the middle of nowhere and give those in need a second chance." He reached for the handrail. "I believe you'll come to the right decision after meeting Raylene. In the meantime, I'll be praying about it."

"Me, too." Jo watched the pastor climb back in his car and slowly drive off. It wasn't until he pulled onto the main road she remembered his jars of honey.

She waited until Pastor Murphy's vehicle was out of sight before Duke and she headed inside.

The one major drawback to the stately Victorian was the lack of air conditioning. The living room air was stagnant and humid. She flipped the switch for the ceiling fan, as she passed through the formal dining room on the way to the large country kitchen.

She eased the swinging door open and stepped into one of her favorite rooms of the house. The tantalizing aroma of fried chicken filled the air.

Delta Childress stood at the counter humming, her back to Jo as she diced cabbage, fresh from the garden.

"Do you need some help?"

"Oh!" Delta clutched her chest. "Jo, you scared me half to death. I've got this under control, although I could use some help frosting the cake. The frosting is over there." She pointed to a bowl on the kitchen table. "Chocolate cake is Emily's favorite. It's my going away gift to her."

"You're so thoughtful. You think of everything, Delta." Jo carried the layered cake to the table. "The jars of honey are selling like hotcakes over in the mercantile."

"I imagine they are. I hid Pastor Murphy's jars of honey on the top shelf of the coat closet, behind the winter gloves."

"Speaking of Pastor Murphy, he just left. I forgot to remind him about the honey." Jo picked up a knife and began frosting the sides of the cake. "He has someone he would like us to meet tomorrow."

Not only was Delta a key member of Jo's household, but she was also Jo's best friend, her sounding board and an exceptional judge of character.

She had shown up on Jo's doorstep not long after she purchased the property, inquiring about a job after word spread around town that she was opening a bed and breakfast.

By the time Delta arrived, Jo had already taken in two women from the prison, both with drug histories. She had her hands full, trying to make sure that the women were comfortable and settling in. She was also up to her eyeballs in readying the mercantile and bakeshop for business, not to mention tending to the gardens.

Jo was certain Delta would bolt when she learned that she was operating a halfway house for the former prison convicts. Instead, she realized God was at work again when she discovered Delta was employed as a cook at the prison.

Never in a million years would Jo have guessed the cheerful, happy-go-lucky woman was a prison cook. Her soft, soothing voice and sympathetic brown eyes spoke acceptance and understanding.

Delta told Jo she currently lived with her niece, Patti, in Divine and confessed that her niece was insisting that her aunt start searching for another job after a recent riot at the prison.

It took all of five minutes for Jo to offer Delta a job. The offer included free room and board, along with a small salary and free meals in exchange for cooking and overseeing the running of the house. Delta promptly accepted.

Jo gave her a tour of the place and introduced her to the two new residents.

The women took to Delta immediately. There was something special about her. By the time Delta left to go home and tell her niece she found a new job and was moving out, Jo was certain God had given her a friend for life.

The women confided in Delta in a way they never did with Jo. Perhaps it was her caring demeanor or her unequivocal acceptance of their pasts. Jo suspected it was a little of both.

Whatever it was, Jo thanked the Lord every day for Delta. It was a friendship made in heaven.

Delta began adding ingredients to the coleslaw, keeping one eye on her friend. "We may have another new resident?"

"I'm not sure. The woman, Raylene, attempted suicide by jumping off *Divine Bridge*. Evan, a local, was on his way to work. He spotted her sitting on the bridge and thought she might be in trouble. He turned around to go back, and that's when he saw her jump."

"I heard about her." Delta set the bowl down. "It's the talk of the town. Patti thinks it was another divine intervention."

"Pastor Murphy thinks so, too." Jo briefly explained what the pastor said. "Raylene was in prison after being convicted in a murder case."

Delta dropped the fork on the counter and wandered over to the table. She plopped down in the chair next to Jo. "What are you going to do?"

"She has nowhere to go. I didn't commit, but told Pastor Murphy I would talk to her tomorrow." Jo sucked in a breath. "I want you to be involved, too. Sometimes you can see things more clearly than I do."

"That's because you have a heart...a big heart. That's what makes you so special, Jo Pepperdine."

"She has nothing, no family, nowhere to go." Jo scraped the side of the frosting bowl. "What if we take her in and she decides to finish what she started? The women here are also in fragile frames of mind. A suicide could be devastating."

"To all of us," Delta pointed out. "I say we talk to her and then go from there."

"I agree." Jo waved her knife at the half-frosted cake. "I better finish frosting the cake. The mercantile is closing soon, and everyone will be heading in for Emily's farewell celebration."

Dinner that evening was bittersweet. Emily, who had come to them after being incarcerated for her role in a string of drug-related robberies, was one of the quieter residents. She was also one of the more thoughtful ones.

Each of the women was required to learn a skill they could take with them, to help find a job, whether it was basic computer skills, gardening, baking or crafting. Nash had even shown a few how to make repairs around the property.

There was also budgeting and a life skills class. Jo taught the women how to open a checking account, balance a checkbook, apply for a job and the list went on.

They each opened an account at the local bank, depositing the small amount of pay Jo gave them each week. The saved money would help them when the time came for them to leave.

Emily had taken a keen interest in woodworking and made each of the other residents a jewelry box. When Jo realized she was almost ready to move out, Emily and she spent the day on the computer, tracking down internet sites where she could market and sell her creations.

The women even managed to set up a small online store and sold a couple of items, giving Emily a much-needed boost in self-confidence.

Although Emily promised to keep in touch and pointed out her leaving would give another woman a second chance at starting over again, Jo was sad to see her go.

It was important to Jo that the women keep in touch, in case one of them began slipping back into their old ways and needed encouragement to get back on track. With Emily's departure, Jo's hopes and dreams of a fresh start for the former convicts was becoming a reality.

After dinner, the women congregated in the living room. It was a touching moment as some of the others presented Emily with going away gifts. More than once, Jo wiped away the tears as she proudly watched the others.

The women turned in early, knowing that tomorrow would be an emotional day.

While Jo got ready for bed, her mind drifted to Raylene Baxter. Her sensible side told her to pass. She had more than enough on her plate without worrying about a possible killer, not to mention a suicide risk, living under her roof.

Her heart told her something completely different. As she drifted off to sleep, she vowed to give Raylene the benefit of the doubt. Jo prayed for Raylene; that God would lead her to the right decision.

Jo tossed and turned all night, her thoughts seesawing between Emily and Raylene. Early the next morning, she crawled out of bed, feeling almost as exhausted as when she crawled in. After a quick shower, she threw on some work clothes.

Today Jo would visit the workshop, check on the beehives, the gardens and then run a quick inventory of the mercantile's merchandise. In between, she would see Emily off and meet Raylene.

She grabbed a pair of socks, and Duke and she headed downstairs.

"...but what if it wasn't?" Jo recognized Nash's deep voice. She wandered into the kitchen and found Delta and Nash standing close together, a look of concern on their faces.

"You're here early. Is everything all right?" Jo asked.

Nash cleared his throat. "I'm sorry to bother you, Jo. It looks like someone tried to break into the store."

# Chapter 3

"The store as in the bakeshop or the store as in the mercantile?" Jo's long and rambling *Second Chance Mercantile* and *Divine Baked Goods Shop* were divided into sections, each with a separate entrance. An interior doorway connected the two, allowing shoppers to pass from one to the other without having to walk outside.

"It was the mercantile. They didn't succeed, but they managed to damage the lock. I'll replace it this morning." Nash led the women out the back door and down the steps.

When they reached the covered porch, Jo peeked in the glass doors of the first building, offering up a prayer of gratitude when she confirmed what Nash had said, that the bakeshop was untouched.

The trio stopped in front of the mercantile entrance where Nash showed her the scratch marks on the front of the door and the damaged lock. "I'll have to install a whole new lock."

"Make it two," Jo said. "I want to make it twice as hard to get in if they try again."

"I'll run back to ask the women if they saw or heard anything." Jo trudged to the back of the building and the women's housing units. It was also the location of the halfway house's common areas. The women were already up and chatting with Emily in the living room.

Jo had forgotten Emily was leaving them. She made her way to the woman's side and gave her a gentle hug. "Today is the big day. Will you have time to stay for breakfast?"

Emily smiled. "Yep. My uncle won't be here until around eleven. He called first thing this morning. He and my aunt are on their way."

"Wonderful. I think Delta was planning to make blueberry pancakes, along with bacon and eggs. We may have to put it off for a short time, though." Jo briefly explained someone had attempted to gain access to the mercantile.

"That's scary." One of the other female residents shook her head. "The thought of someone lurking around gives me the creeps."

Jo assured them that they were safe, but even she was beginning to wonder. It was only a few days ago someone had destroyed their mailbox. Not only destroyed it, but also pulled the post and box right out of the ground.

She reminded the women of the breakfast hour and then returned to the front of the store. Her heart sank when she spied Sheriff Franklin's car parked alongside the mercantile and him standing near the entrance with Nash.

"Good morning, Sheriff Franklin. Is something wrong?"

"I thought we should report the incident," Nash said quietly. "I called the sheriff's office as soon as I noticed the damage."

"Nash told me someone tried to break into the mercantile." The sheriff pointed to the damaged door. "Between the mailbox incident and now this, you might want to consider adding surveillance cameras."

"I thought the same thing," Jo said. "Has anyone else in town reported recent acts of vandalism or break-ins?"

"You're the only one." The sheriff rocked back on his heels. "I'll be completely frank with you Ms. Pepperdine. I admire your determination in trying to help these women and give them a second chance. More than anyone, I understand how people make mistakes. I see it every day in my line of work."

"I appreciate the comment, Sheriff Franklin," Jo said. "These women do deserve a second chance...but then again, don't we all?"

"Yes, we do," he agreed. "Having said that, you need to understand that the Divine residents have some valid concerns about your halfway house. Not only are you inviting criminals."

"Former convicts," Jo corrected.

"Former convicts into your home, you're inviting them into our community. Divine is a small town. The residents don't take kindly to strangers who invite questionable characters to live with them." The sheriff's eyes met Jo's eyes. "Do you understand what I'm saying?"

"Yes. I understand perfectly." Jo clenched her jaw. "I also understand that I'm perfectly within the law to operate this property in the manner I see fit. If you would like to spread the word among the terrified townsfolk, I do screen my residents. They also abide by strict rules, and if they don't, they get the boot."

A slow smile spread across the sheriff's face. "They might not be so fearful if you took the time to visit Divine, maybe drop by the deli for a cup of coffee once in a while and make a point of getting to know some of the residents."

"You're right." Jo couldn't believe she was actually agreeing...agreeing with the man and Marlee, who made a similar comment. "Maybe I should. I plan to be a part of this community for many years to come."

"If you find anything else to add to this morning's incident before I write my report, please don't hesitate to give me a call." Sheriff Franklin tipped his hat and then climbed into his patrol car.

Nash shifted to face Jo. "I have to agree. Maybe you need to get into town to meet more of the locals."

"I suppose. They fear what they don't know." Jo was beginning to warm to the idea. "How can they not like us?" She motioned toward the house. "I'm sure Delta has finished making breakfast."

During breakfast, the women discussed Emily's departure. They listened as she mapped out her plans for the future; how Jo helped her create an online store and her uncle had even managed to add a small workshop to the back of his garage.

She promised she would keep in touch and even invited them to visit her if they ever got down to Oklahoma City.

Jo's heart swelled with pride. She was thrilled that she'd succeeded in her goal of helping the woman get back on her feet, ready to face the world.

Would Emily succeed after leaving Jo's safe, secure environment and was out from under her watchful eye?

Would she fall back into her past life...the one that got her in trouble in the first place?

Or worst of all, would Emily hit the wall and travel the route that poor Raylene Baxter had tried...to enter the darkest of places where she felt she had no choice but to end her life?

Jo mentally shook off the negative thoughts and instead, offered a silent prayer for Emily.

After breakfast, Emily stayed behind to help Delta in the kitchen while she waited for her uncle to arrive.

Jo was taking Emily's departure hard, but Delta was taking it ten times worse. She loved the women, and next to Jo, she was their biggest cheerleader.

"I'm going to take care of some paperwork." Jo headed to her office to catch up on some bills and then wandered back into the kitchen. It was getting close to eleven. Emily's uncle would be arriving at any moment.

She found Emily and Delta sitting at the kitchen table, a box of Kleenex between them and bawling their eyes out.

"Lord have mercy," Jo shook her head. "You two are a hot mess."

Emily giggled through her tears. "Delta and I were reminiscing about the time I burnt her bundt cake, and the kitchen stunk to high heaven."

Delta blew her nose loudly. "I thought we were never gonna get the smell out. That's when Emily decided she would be better off tinkering around in the workshop with Nash."

"And I found my true calling." Emily reached inside her backpack and pulled out two small packages. She handed one to Delta and the other to Jo. "I have something for you. It's not much. I've been working on them for a while now, ever since I knew I would be leaving."

Jo turned the carefully wrapped gift over in her hand. "You didn't have to give us a gift, Emily. We didn't get you anything."

"You're wrong. You gave me the best gift of all. You gave me my life back. You're awesome." Emily sprang from the chair and wrapped her arms around Jo.

Delta joined them, and the women hugged each other, sobbing and laughing.

Nash stepped into the kitchen. "What in the world?"

"Emily gave us a going away gift," Delta hiccupped.

"She gave me one, too and I'll treasure it forever, but it sure as heck didn't make me cry."

Emily laughed. "Liar. I saw your eyes water."

"Sawdust got in my eye," Nash said. "I came in here to tell you that your uncle is here. He's out front talking to Pastor Murphy and another woman. They were heading inside the bakeshop to have a look around."

"Thanks, Nash." Emily motioned with her hands. "Hurry up and open your gifts."

Delta and Jo both removed the delicate tissue paper, revealing a small white box. Jo lifted the lid and pulled out a hand-carved wooden angel.

"This is beautiful." Delta held up her angel. "Look at the detail."

Emily beamed. "Nash helped me track down some small sapphires for the eyes. Do you like them?"

"I love it." Jo swallowed hard, determined not to start bawling again.

"The angels reminded me of the angel story you told me when I first got here," Emily said. "The time you thought an angel rolled you out of bed, so you would see the fire."

Emily clasped her hands tightly, her eyes shining brightly. "What I realized is that you...you two are angels. I think God has a special place in heaven, waiting just for you."

"Thank you, Emily. I'll treasure this forever."

"Now don't go bawlin' again," Nash said gruffly. "Today is a day to celebrate."

"You're right." Emily swiped at the tears and snatched up her backpack. "I'm ready to go."

"Yes, you are," Jo sniffled loudly.

Nash, Emily, Delta and Jo made their way out of the house and to the bakeshop.

A tall man, wearing a ball cap and denim overalls, stood in front of the counter purchasing a package of chocolate chip cookies.

"Uncle Eric."

The man turned at Emily's greeting, a smile lighting his face. "Emily." He wrapped Emily in a bear hug, and then took a step back to study her. "You look wonderful, better than I've seen in years. This place has been good for you."

"Better than good. More like a lifesaver." Emily glanced around. "Where's Aunt Kim?"

"She's outside. She found a big old hound dog, and they're chatting." Emily's uncle turned to Jo. "My wife has yet to meet an animal she doesn't like." He extended his hand. "You must be..."

"Jo. Jo Pepperdine." Jo shook his hand. "You've met my right-hand man, Nash." She took a step back and introduced Delta. "This is the woman who runs the show, Delta Childress."

"Don't let her fool you." Delta warmly shook the uncle's hand. "Jo runs a tight ship around here."

"Thank goodness." Emily shifted her backpack to her other shoulder.

"Let me carry that," Uncle Eric said. "Are you ready to go home?"

"Yes," Emily's eyes twinkled. "I am. I'm ready to go home."

"I'm terrible at good-byes." Delta gave Emily a quick hug. "Behave yourself." Before Emily could reply, Delta darted out the door and disappeared from sight.

Nash was next. He gave Emily a hug. "You keep in touch."

After Nash left, Jo followed Emily and her uncle outdoors where she met Aunt Kim.

"We better get going." Uncle Eric held the door for his wife before opening the van door for Emily. "We have a long drive back to Oklahoma City."

Jo watched Emily climb into the van, her heart heavy and happy all at once. She had a good feeling about the woman's future. It was going to be all right. Emily was going to make it.

She smiled brightly as she waved good-bye until the van drove out of sight. Jo turned to head back indoors when she noticed Delta full out running toward her, a look of panic on her face.

"Jo, you've got to come quick!"

# Chapter 4

"What is it? What happened?"

"It's Gary. Nash found him out near the road. It looks like he's been there for a while." Delta began rambling incoherently.

"Delta, you need to slow down. Gary is out in the gardens."

"No, he's not. He's near the road and unconscious. Nash called an ambulance. They're on the way."

Delta and Jo ran across the side yard, to the front corner of the property. They circled a hedge of bushes where they found Nash kneeling next to Gary, Jo's gardener.

Jo dropped to her knees. "How is he?"

"He's breathing," Nash said. "I've been calling his name, trying to get him to respond."

Jo leaned in. "Gary. It's Jo. Can you hear me?"

He made what was a cross between a sigh and a small gurgling noise.

"I saw his eyes twitch." Delta joined Jo and Nash as she knelt on the ground. "Keep talkin'."

"Gary. I don't know if you can hear me. Nash called an ambulance. Help is on the way. Please hang on."

"Maybe he had a heart attack," she whispered. "Or a stroke."

"There's blood on the back of his head," Nash replied.

"Someone attacked him?" Jo's heart skipped a beat. "Who would attack Gary?"

"Maybe he had some sort of seizure and injured his head when he hit the ground." Delta scrambled to her feet. "I hear the sirens. I'll wave them down."

She flew around the side of the hedge and disappeared from sight.

While they waited, Jo continued talking in a soft, low voice, encouraging Gary to hang on, that the EMTs were almost there. She reached for Gary's calloused hand and gave it a gentle squeeze.

"Now we can't have you conking out on us, Gary Stein. We need your expertise in the gardens. Delta made you a special batch of oatmeal raisin cookies yesterday, one of your favorites."

Gary, a retired farmer, volunteered his time and knowledge a couple of days a week to help keep up with the planting, weeding and harvesting. In exchange, he was free to take as many fruits and vegetables as he wanted, along with his choice of Delta's freshly baked goods.

It was a win-win situation for Jo and for Gary, a widower, whom she suspected was lonely. He was also one of the few Divine residents who didn't view Jo and the residents as bad pennies.

A movement caught Jo's eye as Delta, accompanied by two EMTs, raced toward them. "He's over here."

Nash joined the women, and the trio hovered off to the side. All the while, Jo prayed for Gary, that help had arrived in time.

"What happened?" One of the EMTs turned his attention to them.

"I don't know," Nash said. "I came out here a short time ago to check on Gary. When I got here, I found him on the ground unconscious."

"There's a deep wound on the back of his neck." The EMT gently examined Gary's head. "It appears he may have suffered a concussion. Do you know if he has any existing medical conditions?"

"Not that we're aware of," Jo said. Unfortunately, she knew little of Gary's background, other than he had once farmed acres of fields in the Divine area, having inherited the property from his parents and grandparents, going generations back. He now leased the land and instead, spent his free time helping Jo.

The EMT asking the questions excused himself and hurried off. He returned a short time later, carrying a portable stretcher. The men gently loaded Gary onto the stretcher and then carried him to the waiting ambulance.

Nash, Delta and Jo followed behind. "Where will you take him?"

"To Mercy Hospital. We don't allow passengers, but someone can follow us. It would be helpful if you could contact the immediate family and meet us at the hospital."

A crowd gathered near the ambulance, talking in hushed voices as they watched the EMTs load Gary into the ambulance. They shut the back doors and climbed into the cab, turning the lights and sirens on as soon as they drove onto the road.

"I'll follow them to the hospital," Nash offered. "As soon as I know anything, I'll give you a call."

"That would be great."

Nash grabbed the keys from the workshop before climbing into his truck and driving off.

Delta eyed the onlookers and then whispered in Jo's ear. "We best stick to the truth, that we don't know what happened to Gary."

"I agree," Jo whispered back. "I'll take care of the crowd."

Delta returned to the house while Jo addressed the onlookers. "Gary, our part-time gardener, collapsed out front. Nash is on the way to the hospital to be with him."

The crowd dispersed and Jo waited until they had gone back inside before returning to the spot where Nash found Gary.

She circled the hedge before starting back toward the house when someone called her name. "Jo!"

It was Pastor Murphy and a woman Jo had never met before. She waited for them to join her.

"I heard Gary Stein is on his way to the hospital."

"Yes. We're not sure what happened. Nash found him out front near the hedge."

"I hope he's all right."

"Me, too." Jo nodded at the pastor before turning her attention to the woman, her eyes drawn to her somber, haunted expression. *Raylene.*

If she had to guess, the woman was younger than Jo, maybe in her early to mid-forties. She was medium build and height, but other than her expression, nothing stood out as particularly memorable.

"I think we may have caught you at a bad time." Pastor Murphy smiled apologetically. "Raylene and I were just shopping in the mercantile." He waved the bag of clothes he was holding.

"No. No. It's all right," Jo said. "Please. Come inside. I'll start a pot of coffee. While you're here, you can grab your jars of honey."

Jo led the pastor and Raylene up the porch steps, through the house and into the kitchen where they found Delta buzzing back and forth.

She did a double take when she spied the pastor and the woman. "Pastor Murphy. I plum forgot you were stopping by today." Delta hurried to the closet and returned with two large jars of honey. "Our honey has been selling like hotcakes ever since we put it out yesterday. Why, I told Jo we could double the price and it would still fly off the shelves."

"Thank you." Pastor Murphy took the jars. "How much do I owe you?"

"How about another clothing drive?" Jo asked.

"It's a deal. If not for you, half the women in Smith County wouldn't have an excuse to clean out their closets and go shopping."

"Have a seat." Delta pulled out a chair and motioned Raylene to sit down. "I didn't catch your name."

"Where are my manners? Raylene Baxter, this is Jo...Joanna Pepperdine, owner of the *Second Chance Mercantile* and *Divine Baked Goods Shop*." The pastor nodded toward Delta. "And this is Jo's right-hand gal, Delta Childress, one of the best cooks and bakers in all of Smith County, maybe even the State of Kansas."

"Sawyer, you're too kind." Delta clutched the edge of her apron. "I suppose you're flattering me so that I'll make another batch of my very cherry hand pies."

The pastor patted his paunch. "I do love your pies, Delta."

"I started a fresh pot of coffee. I don't have cherry pie on hand, but I do have a lemon cake fresh from the oven."

"If it's anything like your lemon pie, we're in for a real treat."

Jo helped Delta carry the coffee and cake plates to the table before settling into a chair across from Raylene. "So you were shopping at the mercantile?"

"Yes." The pastor hesitated, choosing his words carefully. "While we were here, I thought I would introduce you to Raylene. She's a little down on her luck, and is in the market for a place to stay," he said delicately. "Naturally, I thought of you since you're in the business of helping strangers."

"I'm homeless," Raylene said bluntly. "I don't think you'll want to offer me a place to stay. I just got out of prison. I'm a convicted felon."

Jo, taken aback by Raylene's bluntness, arched her brow. "I..." She decided the best approach was to match the woman's directness. "Did you kill someone?"

"No, but my best friend and business partner, Brock, is dead. His death haunts me every day." Raylene gazed directly into Jo's eyes. "I see what's going on here. I heard about this place while I was locked up in the joint. This is a halfway house. I already know that you don't take women convicted of murder, so I don't see why I'm here and why we're wasting everyone's time."

Pastor Murphy's jaw dropped.

Delta, who so far remained silent, spoke, her voice calm yet firm. "Sugar, you'll attract more flies with honey. Listen, you've had a hard time. We get it, but if you're trying to convince Ms. Jo that you're a good fit for a spot here you are failing miserably."

Raylene slowly shifted her gaze and her expression softened. Jo could've sworn the woman almost cracked a smile. Almost. "I like you."

"I might like you, too," Delta replied. "Now. Shall we start again, this time with you answering Jo's question as honestly as possible?"

Raylene nodded. "Yes, ma'am."

"Delta. My name is Delta."

"Delta, ma'am. My friend and I managed to put ourselves in a dangerous situation. Someone we trusted tricked us, and that person arranged for us to meet with some gang members, some bad people. By the time we realized what was going down, it was too late, so I came up with a plan to extricate ourselves as expeditiously as possible. My plan backfired."

"So you're saying you didn't kill Brock," Jo said.

"Brock was jumped and during the struggle, he was shot. I freaked out and took off. Did I pull the trigger? No. It didn't matter. The jury decided I was partially to blame for my partner's death. Did I come up with the plan that killed my best friend? Without a doubt."

"I see." Jo sipped her coffee, eyeing the woman over the rim. Pastor Murphy was right. There was something about the woman, something different. Maybe it was her directness. Maybe it was the raw emotion in her words and her demeanor.

She was a fighter, which surprised Jo since the woman had jumped off *Divine Bridge* in an attempt to end her life. "Pastor Murphy said you jumped off

*Divine Bridge* and lived. Quite a feat since it doesn't have the leap of death nickname for nothing."

"I did." Raylene nodded. "I had no money, unless you call the measly seventy-five bucks on a debit card charging twenty percent interest and a monthly fee of ten bucks money. All I had were the clothes on my back. I have no family, no friends and nowhere to go."

"So you decided to jump off the bridge to commit suicide and God decided he had other plans," Jo said softly. "I heard the story...it sounds like a divine intervention."

Raylene stared at Jo, unblinking for several long seconds. It was so quiet at the table; you could've heard a pin drop.

The woman's face crumpled. In the blink of an eye, she regained her composure. "Maybe."

It took all of two seconds for Jo to decide whether she was going to invite Raylene Baxter to stay.

# Chapter 5

Before Jo could announce her decision, she felt a sharp kick under the table, courtesy of Delta, who was giving her "the look." "If you'll excuse Delta and me for a moment, we need to have a word in private."

She abruptly stood. Delta followed suit, and the women stepped out the back door and into the backyard.

Jo waited until they were a safe distance from the house. "I know I'm breaking one of my own rules by inviting Raylene to live with us, but there's something about her."

"There's something about her. Something not right." Delta shivered. "I feel it in my bones. You don't feel it? Like she's hiding something."

"I didn't get that impression at all. Raylene is a perfect example of someone who was dealt a bad hand and needs a second chance. She doesn't strike me as trying to hide anything."

"Then you aren't looking hard enough." Delta pointed at her eyes. "You got to look at the eyes. The lights are on, but the curtains are closed."

The women went back and forth, with Jo rattling off the reasons she believed Raylene was a good fit for the halfway house. Delta was quick to shoot down every one of them.

She ended the discussion by reminding Jo that she was breaking her own rule if she invited the woman to live with them. "Plus, the other women, they know the rules. How do you think they'll react when they find out a possible killer is living among us?"

Delta had a valid point. Jo's number one priority was not only giving the women a second chance but also keeping them safe, something they hadn't felt for many years. *She* was responsible for their safety.

"Ugh! I hate it when you're right." Jo stomped her foot in frustration. She started toward the door and abruptly stopped. A sudden thought, a possible compromise popped into her head.

"What if we offered to let Raylene spend a couple of nights, long enough for Pastor Murphy to find somewhere else for her to go?"

Delta stubbornly shook her head. "The rules…"

"Yes. I know my own rules, but how will you feel if you find out she's living on the streets or even worse, returns to *Divine Bridge* to finish what she started?"

Jo could see that Delta was considering her words and pressed on. "Think about it…she has nowhere to go. No one who cares what happens to her. She's at the end of the road. Why else would she try to end her life? Do you want Raylene's death on your conscience?"

The women's eyes met, Jo's eyes pleading her case to her closest friend, whose opinion she valued as much as her own.

Delta sucked in a breath. "Fine. You win. I'll go along with asking her to join us, but only temporarily, and I'm gonna be keeping my guns handy, just in case. I would advise you to do the same."

Jo impulsively hugged her friend. "We're making the right decision. You'll see. Raylene will probably be the best resident we've had yet."

"We'll see all right," Delta grumbled. "Don't say I didn't warn you. Let's head back inside before I change my mind again."

"It'll be fine." Jo motioned for Delta to go first and then followed her up the steps and into the kitchen.

Pastor Murphy shot them an inquiring look, while Raylene fiddled with the handle of her coffee cup, looking like she wished she were anywhere but there.

"Sorry for the brief intermission." Jo resumed her place at the table. "There's no sense in beating around the bush. Delta and I, along with Nash, take our decisions regarding residents seriously. The women who live here are all in similar situations." She motioned to Raylene. "As you correctly pointed out, I don't take in women convicted of murder, manslaughter or any situation involving the taking of another's life."

Jo paused, searching for the right words, ones that wouldn't put Raylene on the defensive, yet strong enough to let her know they would be watching, that she would be offering her a helping hand, but with some strings attached.

"We're not sure you're a good fit for the farm. Having said that, we understand you have nowhere to go." Jo focused her attention on Raylene, who lifted her chin and met Jo's unwavering gaze. "I would like to offer you a place to stay since one of the residents left this morning. It would be on a temporary basis."

Jo turned her attention to the pastor. "In the meantime, I would ask that Pastor Murphy works on finding you a more permanent arrangement."

"That seems fair," Pastor Murphy agreed. "I understand this will put you in a predicament with the other residents, and thank you for bending the rules."

"I appreciate the offer," Raylene said quietly. "My pride tells me to refuse, but common sense is getting in the way. I'll take you up on your generous offer while Pastor Murphy tries to find somewhere else for me to go."

"It's a deal." Jo downed the last of her coffee. "I have some things to take care of. I want to call Nash, to see if he has word yet on Gary's condition."

She stood, her signal that the meeting was over.

Delta, who remained standing after returning to the kitchen, set her empty coffee cup in the sink. "Jo will go over the house rules. The kitchen rules are a little different."

"Delta rules the roost in the kitchen," Jo joked. "Don't come in uninvited. If you mess it up, clean it up. We eat dinner at six on the dot and don't even think about questioning what's on the table."

"You eat what we have, or you go hungry," Delta quipped.

Raylene smiled. "You won't have to worry about me complaining or bothering you in the kitchen. I can burn water."

Delta returned the smile. "Then we'll get along just fine."

"Don't you want to hear my story?"

"Yes," Jo nodded. "You can share it tonight at dinner. There are no secrets among the residents. Because of the obvious circumstances for you being here, it's important that everyone knows everyone else's incarceration history."

"I see," Raylene said. "So I guess I better get my story straight."

Jo gave her a direct stare. "Lying about your past is grounds for immediate removal. You don't have to elaborate. You can give us the basics, but be warned that I can and will verify what you tell us, in addition to what Pastor Murphy has already told me."

Raylene hung her head. "I was kidding. Of course, I'll be honest. It's not the proudest time in my life."

"We all have those times." Jo's tone softened. "This is all about second chances. You have to start your new journey by facing your past and telling the truth."

Raylene and Jo walked Pastor Murphy to his car. Before he left, he promised to start that very day finding Raylene a permanent home.

Jo shaded her eyes and watched him pull onto the street before turning to Raylene, who was still holding the bag of items the pastor purchased for her at the mercantile. "Let me show you where you'll be staying. Emily cleaned her unit before she left, so I'm sure the place is ready for you to move into."

The women wandered past the building, to the back and the residents' units. The door to Emily's former home was unlocked, and Jo led Raylene inside. "Remind me to give you the key to this unit. It's on my desk."

Jo gave her a brief tour of the cozy unit. All six units - or apartments - were identical. Each apartment included a twin bed, a nightstand, a four-drawer dresser and small wall-mounted television.

"Sandwiched in between the units is the common area. There's a living room in case you want to hang out with the other women, along with two shared bathrooms with cabinets in each. You'll be allowed to pick an empty cabinet, and I suggest you keep your toiletries locked inside. There is also a small kitchenette with a microwave, fridge and cooktop.

As I mentioned earlier, dinner is at six and Delta is a stickler for keeping the dinner schedule."

Raylene nodded occasionally as Jo led her from the unit to the common area. She asked a question or two, but let Jo do most of the talking.

"Since the others are working in different areas of the property, we'll do proper introductions when we gather for dinner." Jo glanced at her watch, certain that Nash would have an update on Gary's condition by now.

"I need to make a quick telephone call."

"Of course." Raylene wandered around the common area, inspecting her temporary home while Jo plucked her cell phone from her back pocket and dialed Nash's number. He didn't answer, so she left him a brief message, asking him to call with an update on Gary's condition.

She ended the call and slid the phone back in her pocket, her thoughts still on Gary. Was the attempted break-in at the mercantile and Gary's incident related?

Jo had a sinking feeling that they, along with the destruction of her mailbox, were somehow related. "I'm going to take a look around the back gardens. You can tag along if you like. It will give you a feel for the lay of the land. We'll also stop by Nash's workshop for a quick peek inside."

The women leisurely strolled down the two-lane dirt path, leading along the fence line, past the smaller of Jo's two gardens. The first garden contained carrots, radishes and potatoes.

The larger garden, farther back was where Jo grew sunflowers, along with her corn, rhubarb, lettuce and cabbage.

Before purchasing the property, Jo knew very little about growing a garden, but she knew if she were to implement her plan, she needed to learn...and fast. After Gary's arrival, Jo spent time with him, eager to learn what it took to grow a garden, one large enough to sell the produce.

Gary had a green thumb and seemed to love helping Jo as much as she loved having him around. She swallowed the lump in her throat and silently prayed that when Nash called, he would have good news.

"We have bees out back. They make some fine tasting honey," Jo explained. The women gave the bee boxes a wide berth before rounding the corner where the silo stood sentinel, guarding the gardens.

Jo pointed out the various vegetables as they walked. Her impression of Raylene was that the woman was an excellent listener, a trait Jo appreciated since she wasn't much for idle chatter. Delta was the one with a gift for gab.

Raylene asked all of the right questions and appeared genuinely interested in Jo's operation.

The tour of the grounds ended near the front and the spot where Nash found Gary. Jo grew somber, the image of poor Gary burned in her memory.

"Is this where you found your...friend?"

"Yes." Jo solemnly nodded. "He was lying right here, face up. Nash said there was blood on the back of his head."

"I see." Raylene took a couple of steps to the right, studying the layout of the front yard. There was something sticking out near the corner of the hedge.

Raylene knelt down for a closer inspection, careful not to touch it. "Joanna, I think I found something."

# Chapter 6

Jo rushed to Raylene's side. "This is one of our garden hoes. Gary must've taken it from the garden shed. He probably stopped by here to grab the wheelbarrow and some gardening tools before heading out back."

"You don't see it? Raylene pointed to the metal blade.

"See what?"

"The splotches."

Jo sank to her knees, her eyes narrowing as she studied the metal blade. "Is that..." Her voice trailed off.

"It looks like blood."

Jo reached for the handle. Raylene's hand shot out to stop her. "Don't touch it. This may be potential evidence."

"You're right." Jo snatched her hand back. "We need to call the police to come out here and take this in as potential evidence."

Jo slipped her cell phone from her back pocket and searched for the sheriff's non-emergency number before pressing the call button. She inwardly cringed when Evelyn McBride, answered.

"Smith County emergency dispatch, Evelyn McBride speaking."

"Yes, this is Joanna Pepperdine, over on 712 D Road. One of my workers was injured this morning. I think he was attacked and would like someone to stop by to take a look at what I believe may be potential evidence."

"You've got to be..." Evelyn caught herself and abruptly stopped. She cleared her throat. "I'll dispatch one of the deputies to your location.

Someone should be there within the next half an hour."

Jo thanked the woman and disconnected the call. She'd just placed the cell phone back in her pocket, when it let out a small chirp. Nash had sent her a text.

She held the phone away in an attempt to read Nash's message. "Thank God." Jo pressed a hand to her chest, sudden tears filling her eyes.

"Good news, I hope," Raylene said.

"Yes. Gary has a concussion, but it looks like he'll be all right. The doctors are going to keep him overnight for observation." Jo's relief was quickly followed by a wave of seething anger.

Someone was determined to harass Jo and her employees, and Jo was equally determined to figure out who it was. "We're going to get to the bottom of this." She stepped away from the hedge and marched across the driveway.

Raylene jogged along beside her in an attempt to keep up.

"Someone destroyed my mailbox, attempted to break into the mercantile and now Gary's attack. It appears the culprit is getting more brazen and more dangerous with each incident."

"Do you have any enemies, anyone in town who may have it in for you?" Raylene asked.

"There is one woman, a local named Debbie Holcomb, who I heard doesn't care for us. An anonymous complaint was filed against me, claiming I'm running an unlicensed bed and breakfast."

"Well, there you go," Raylene said breathlessly. "Someone is trying to destroy your business. Now you just have to try to figure out who."

"That will be nearly impossible."

"I'm not trying to tell you what to do, but if I were you, I would start snooping around town, asking questions."

"The only person I know is Marlee. She owns *Divine Delicatessen* in town," Jo said.

"I remember seeing the place on my way through town. Divine is small...small enough where everybody knows everybody else. The deli would be a great place to start."

"Or I'll leave it up to the authorities," Jo said. "If I start snooping around Divine, I'm sure to make even more enemies than I apparently already have."

The women slowed their pace as they drew close to the mercantile.

"You could sit back and wait to see if or when someone comes after you again," Raylene shrugged. "If I were in your shoes, I would make a move; try to figure out who is doing this."

Jo reached for the door handle. "What were you...some sort of private investigator?"

"Not quite. I do have a teensy bit of investigative background, which came in handy in my previous line of work."

"Huh." Jo wrinkled her nose, eyeing her houseguest with interest. "I can't wait for dinner tonight, to hear your story."

"It's not that exciting. My career choice was kind of by accident," Raylene mumbled under her breath.

"I don't believe in accidents." Jo opened the door. "You've already been inside the mercantile, but I need to check on the women working here today to make sure they don't need anything."

Jo briefly chatted with the two women working, and then they made their way into the bakeshop. Off to one side was a small seating area. On the other side were several display cases.

Delta woke early each morning, and with the help of two of the women, they whipped up an array of tempting baked goods. The shop sported a small prep area in the back, but Delta created all of her masterpieces in Jo's state-of-the-art commercial kitchen.

Despite Jo's admission that she didn't know the town's residents, she was certain many of them visited the bakery on a regular basis to purchase some of Delta's delectable goodies.

"Those look tasty." Raylene pointed to a tray of brownie bites.

"They are delicious," Jo said. "Delta makes some of the best brownies on the planet. Would you like to try one?"

"I...I'm sure you would rather sell them."

"I think we can spare one small brownie." Jo winked at Sherry, the woman behind the counter.

"And they are extra delish today." Sherry plucked a waxed paper from the box on top of the display, reached inside and removed a brownie. "I don't know how Delta does it."

Raylene thanked Sherry for the brownie and nibbled the edge. "Oh. These are delicious." She took another bite, this time bigger. "I sure wish I knew how to bake."

"Delta will teach you," Sherry smiled. "So you're the new girl on the block. You're taking Emily's place."

"Temporarily," Raylene said. "Until I can find a new place to live."

"Welcome to what we nicknamed *Second Chance*. We're all convinced Jo is an angel. You'll love living here and will never want to leave."

A warmth swept through Jo at Sherry's glowing praise. "Now don't go making me sound too good."

"But you are." Sherry shrugged. "Anyway, welcome to *Second Chance*."

"Thank you." Raylene lifted the brownie. "And thank you for the brownie. I'll see you later?"

"You bet."

A customer approached, and the women stepped out of the store.

Raylene waited for the door to shut behind them. "She was nice."

"All of the women here are nice. We're one nice, big family."

"I wish…" Raylene's voice trailed off, and Jo knew she was going to say she wished she could stay, but Delta's warning, how Jo was breaking one of her own rules, ran through her head.

Fair was fair. Hopefully, Pastor Murphy would find somewhere for Raylene to go, somewhere that would give her a fair shake at a fresh start.

Before Jo could answer, a patrol car pulled into the parking lot. This time it was Deputy Brian Franklin, the junior Franklin.

Jo and Raylene waited for him to join them on the porch.

The young deputy nodded at Raylene and turned to Jo. "Heard you may have some new information on Gary's injury."

"I'm sure you heard Nash found him unconscious this morning."

"Yes, ma'am."

The trio began making their way to the hedge near the front. "Raylene and I were touring the property and found a hoe. There appears to be blood on the blade."

"On my way here, I called the hospital to check on Gary. Although he took a nasty clunk to the back of his head, the doctors say he's going to be all right."

"Yes, I spoke with Nash and he said the same thing." Jo led the deputy to the hoe. "We haven't touched it."

Deputy Franklin circled the hoe before bending down for a closer inspection. "You're right. I do believe there is blood on the blade." He pulled a handkerchief from his pocket and carefully wrapped it around the wooden handle. "I'll take this to the station for evidence. I'm assuming you would like the matter investigated."

"Yes. Someone is targeting me…targeting us and I want to find out who it is," Jo said. "They're trying to scare me, and it's not going to work."

"It does appear that way," the deputy agreed. "I heard someone tried to break into the mercantile. Could be the same person."

"That's what I was thinking."

Raylene, who had remained silent so far, spoke. "If you think about it, they probably tried to break into the mercantile early this morning. After giving up, they were on their way out and ran into Gary."

Jo picked up. "They panicked when they saw him, grabbed the hoe and whacked him on the back of the head."

"Did you notice anything else, other than the hoe?" Deputy Franklin asked.

"No, but we weren't looking," Jo said.

The deputy propped the garden hoe against the shed and circled the hedge, his sharp gaze studying the road, the fence line and the fields beyond. "It would be fairly easy for someone to sneak across the fields here along the property line and then take off down this main road."

The deputy opened the door to the shed, looked inside and then closed it. "I'll write up the report and stop by later for you to sign it. In the meantime, I would be careful not to wander around after dark on your own, until we figure out who is causing you the trouble."

"I appreciate your help." Jo, accompanied by Raylene, followed the deputy to his patrol car. She watched him place the garden tool in the trunk. "The sooner we can get to the bottom of this, the better. It seems whoever is responsible for these acts of vandalism and now this attack is getting bolder."

"I'll make it a priority, Ms. Pepperdine." The deputy promised to contact Jo as soon as he finished his investigation.

Jo thanked him for stopping by and turned to Raylene. "It's my turn to work at the mercantile. First, I want to chat with Sherry." She waited for the younger woman to step inside the bakeshop and they approached Sherry, who was standing behind the counter.

"I'm beginning to suspect Gary was attacked, and whoever tried to break into the mercantile might also be responsible for his injuries."

A customer stepped inside, and Jo waited until they wandered to the other side of the bakery. "Do you recall hearing or seeing anything early this morning?"

"No." Sherry's expression grew thoughtful. "I take that    back. Around six-thirty, I heard a dull *clunk,* but it could've been Nash. He sometimes borrows the garbage cans for the workshop."

"Did you look outside when you heard the noise?"

"No. I was still half-asleep. I remember rolling over to look at my alarm clock, though. That's how I know what time it was."

"Anything else?" Jo prompted.

"That was it, and I'm not sure it was anything. Like I said, sometimes Nash borrows one of the cans. Maybe you should check with him."

Jo thanked Sherry for the information, and she and Raylene wandered out of the bakery and into the mercantile. Business was brisk, and the changeover from Julie to Jo took a few minutes.

Julie quickly counted the contents of the register while Jo watched. "Where are you headed now?" Delta was in charge of the women's work schedules, and a copy of each day's schedule was posted on the bulletin board in the common area's "living room."

"I was supposed to help Nash in the workshop, but I don't think he's back from the hospital yet," Julie said. "Is there something else you would like me to do?"

Nash was nitpicky when it came to his workshop. He didn't allow anyone inside unless he was there. Not that Jo could blame him. There were several heavy-duty power tools and other equipment. Unless a person was skilled at operating the special machinery, it was an accident waiting to happen.

"Maybe you could run by the smaller of the gardens to see if there are any vegetables that are ready to be picked. With Gary out of commission, we may have to tweak the schedules until further notice."

"Of course." Julie turned to go.

"Oh!" Jo held up her hand. "You didn't happen to hear anything early this morning, say around six-thirty where maybe someone was messing around behind the store."

"No." Julie rubbed the palms of her hands together. "I woke up around seven."

"No thumps or other odd noises?"

"Nope." Julie shook her head.

"Thanks, Julie. And thanks for running by the gardens."

The store was busy. Jo put Raylene to work, helping the customers near the back and with the fitting rooms. She didn't notice Nash until he was standing in front of the counter. His flushed face bore an anxious expression.

"You're back," Jo said. "How is Gary?"

"I have some good and bad news."

# Chapter 7

The color drained from Jo's face, a feeling of dread dropping like lead in the pit of her stomach. She said the first thing that popped into her head. "Gary is going to be okay..."

"Yes. He'll be laid up for a few days. The doctors are going to have a tough time," Nash said. "They'll probably have to tie him to the bed. He's already threatening to leave."

Jo pressed the palm of her hand to her forehead. "Thank God. We can cover the gardens for as long as Gary needs to heal."

"He's all fired up, insisting he's going to be out of the hospital by the end of the day."

"I'll run by the hospital a little later, after my shift ends, to check on him. Maybe I can talk some sense into him."

"Good luck with that. The good news is we'll have to pick him up to give him a ride home so he won't get very far." Nash reached in his pants pocket and pulled out a sheet of paper. "He's worried about the gardens. He jotted down a few notes and asked me to give them to you."

Jo glanced at the sheet. "Julie is on her way to check on them now. I am a little concerned about the bees since Gary is the official beekeeper."

"We can handle the beehives. I can keep an eye on them until Gary is back on his feet."

Jo thanked Nash for following Gary to the hospital and for the update. A customer approached, and Jo turned her attention to running the store.

The mercantile was busier than normal for a Thursday. When Jo questioned one of the shoppers, they mentioned the annual *Geographic Center Supernatural Festival* being held at a farm a few miles away.

Raylene, who was helping Jo package purchases, waited until the woman left. "Did you hear that? A supernatural festival. What did she mean about this area being the geographic center?"

"It's the center point of the lower forty-eight United States," Jo said. "I watched a show about it some time ago. Some claim there are supernatural powers associated with the center of anything."

"Like angel supernatural powers?" Raylene's eyes widened.

Jo thought back to her own unexplained incident, where she felt she was being shoved out of bed in the middle of the night only to discover one of her outlets was smoldering. "Quite possibly. I...believe in God. I believe in angels. It's in the Bible." Jo quoted a verse.

*"For he will command his angels concerning you to guard you in all your ways; they will lift you up in their hands, so that you will not strike your foot against a stone."* **Psalm 91: 11-12 NIV**

"I believe in angels, too," Raylene said. "God's angels saved my life. As soon as I get a chance, I'm going to track down the man who was there when the angels rescued me. Did you hear that they disappeared as soon as they placed me on the banks?"

"Yes, I did." Before Jo could elaborate, another customer approached the checkout. The next couple of hours flew by. Raylene was a huge help to Jo, and she was thankful the woman was there.

Finally, it was time for Julie to take over again, for the last shift before the store closed.

Nash, Delta and Jo were the only ones with keys to the bakeshop and mercantile, so Jo asked Delta to help close for the night before grabbing her keys and heading to the hospital to check on Gary.

When she arrived, she found Gary in his room and alone. He looked surprised to see her. "You didn't have to drive all the way over here."

"I wanted to, and I want to tell you how sorry I am." Jo perched on the edge of the chair next to Gary's bed. "I feel terrible. Nash told me you're ready to leave, but you need to stay until the doctors release you."

"I'm fit as a fiddle," Gary insisted.

"Gary." Jo slowly shook her head.

"Fine," he grumbled. "I'll stay for the night, but that's it. I'm leaving in the morning."

They discussed the hospital stay, Jo's gardens and then the subject drifted to Gary's incident.

"Tell me everything you remember."

"It was early this morning. I wanted to get a jump on the summer heat and decided to work in the big garden. I had just opened the shed and noticed a funny smell. I stepped inside to have a look around when I heard a *thump* from behind me," Gary said. "I turned around. Next thing I know, I'm in the ambulance on the way to the hospital."

Adding a padlock to the shed was another item on Jo's to-do list, but she hadn't gotten around to it. "You think there was someone hiding inside the shed?" Jo asked.

"Maybe. I wish I could remember more."

They chatted until one of the nurses stopped by to check on him. She told Jo the doctor hadn't made a decision on Gary's release. They would know more in the morning after he had time to rest.

"I better get going. It's getting late." She promised Gary she would check on him in the morning and if the doctor released him, someone would return to give him a ride home.

During the quiet ride back, Jo thought about Gary's comment, how he heard a *thump* and couldn't remember anything after that.

Sherry had said the same thing...how she heard a *clunk* early that morning. Not long after, Nash discovered someone had tried to break into the mercantile.

Jo was certain whoever tried to break-in was the same person who attacked Gary. Now all she needed to do was figure out who it was. Or better yet, the authorities needed to figure out who was targeting her - and soon!

She made it back to the house at five fifty-nine with barely enough time to wash up before joining the others in the dining room.

Delta's dinner consisted of grilled pork chops, baked potatoes with a side of coleslaw and corn on the cob. Michelle, one of the residents, helped Delta carry the platters of food and dinner plates to the table.

After everyone was seated, the women bowed their heads, and Jo prayed: "Dear Heavenly Father. Thank you for giving us one more day on earth to celebrate the gift of your Son, Jesus. Lord, we have some special prayers this evening. First, and foremost, we pray for Gary, for the injuries he sustained this morning. We pray for his complete healing. We also pray for our friend, Emily, for her new life in Oklahoma City, that you keep her close to you."

"Today, we bring another new friend to the table, Raylene. Lord, we pray for Raylene, for a perfect home for our new friend. We pray for blessings in her life. Thank you for hearing our prayers. Thank you for this bountiful harvest of food. Thank you most of all, for your Son, our Savior. Amen."

"Amen." A chorus of amens went up.

Jo rose to her feet. "Before we start eating, I would like all of you to say 'hello' to Raylene. Raylene is from the women's penitentiary. She's only going to be with us temporarily, we're not sure how long. We'll give her a chance to share her story as soon as we finish dinner."

The women smiled politely, and greeted her.

"I'm happy to be here," she said.

"Welcome to the best place on the planet." Michelle eased a grilled pork chop on her plate and passed the platter to Julie. "How is Mr. Gary?"

"He's itching to leave the hospital, so I think he'll be all right. The doctors are going to keep him overnight," Jo said. "Now that we're all together, I need to know if any of you heard anything or saw anything this morning, other than Sherry and Julie, who I already talked to."

Jo briefly explained her theory, that the attempted break-in and Gary's attack were linked. "Raylene and I discovered blood on a hoe, not far from where Nash found Gary."

Delta's fork clattered on her plate. "So someone did attack Gary."

"It appears that way."

"This is too much," Delta said. "It's one thing right after another...the mangled mailbox, the attempted break-in and now Gary's attack. Maybe we should implement a nightly watch."

"I hope it doesn't come to that." Jo sighed heavily. She'd actually thought the same thing. She was at a loss and starting to feel her home was no longer the safe haven she'd worked so hard to create.

The women threw out different theories of who might be responsible for the frightening incidents. They all agreed on one thing...it was someone who was determined to harass Jo and/or the residents.

"I think we need to head right to town and start asking questions," Delta slammed her palm on the table. "We're gonna start with that witch, Debbie Holcomb."

"Marlee said we should make a point to get to know the residents of Divine. Maybe they'll realize we're good people and there's nothing to fear," Jo said.

"It sure wouldn't hurt," Delta said. "I could use a few things in town. Why don't we head there after breakfast tomorrow?"

"Or eat breakfast at the deli," Julie suggested. "It won't look as suspicious."

"Oh, it's gonna look suspicious no matter what we do," Jo said. "But Julie is right. Let's have breakfast at the deli."

With a plan in place and Jo feeling better that at least she was trying to do something, they began discussing covering Gary's gardening duties. Delta promised she would revise the work schedule after dinner, adding Raylene to the rotation.

The meal ended and everyone helped clear the table while Jo brewed a pot of decaf coffee and Delta loaded the dishwasher. "I made a cherry cobbler for dessert."

"It looks delicious." Jo carried the cobbler to the table while Delta grabbed a stack of dessert plates.

The women settled in around the table, enjoying Delta's divine cobbler when Jo turned to Raylene. "Well, Raylene. It's your turn. How did you end up at Central?"

Raylene shifted uncomfortably as all eyes turned to her. "My mother died young. My dad tried to raise my siblings and me. He couldn't handle all of us. I finally decided at sixteen, I was old enough to get along on my own."

"That got you in trouble," Sherry predicted.

"Yes." Raylene nodded. "Long story short, I got in with the wrong crowd, spent a few years in foster homes. About fifteen years ago, I met my friend, Brock. He was the manager at a local fast food restaurant. Brock gave me my first real job. He saved my life, and I ended up being responsible for the end of his."

"Did you murder your friend?" Delta asked.

"The jury convicted me of being an accomplice. That's how I ended up in prison. We were business partners. The business was legit, thanks to Brock. We were on assignment over in Kansas City, working undercover if you will. We thought we finally had our guy, but it was a trap. By the time we realized what was happening, it was too late. I came up with a plan to get us out of a tight spot.

Unfortunately, it backfired, and Brock died. I ran away and left him there to die."

Tears welled up in Raylene's eyes, and her lower lip trembled. Jo reached across the table and squeezed her hand. "I'm sorry, Raylene. We all make mistakes. Now it's time to look to the future and give yourself a second chance."

Raylene nodded, the tears running unchecked down her cheeks. "Excuse me." She scrambled out of her chair. It hit the floor with a loud *thud* as she darted out of the dining room.

Seconds later, the front porch door slammed.

"That's awful," Sherry whispered.

"I don't think I could live with myself," Michelle added.

"She didn't either," Jo said.

"I thought murderers were a no-go here," Julie said.

"Yeah." One of the other women nodded her agreement. "She could be lying. What if she's a killer?"

"I..." Jo shot Delta a helpless look. "Yes. Those are the rules."

Delta jumped in to help. "It's only temporary...until Pastor Murphy can find a home for Raylene."

Sherry gazed toward the front of the house. "She's the one. She's the one who jumped off *Divine Bridge* the other day. I heard about her."

"Yes," Jo said. "I was afraid if we turned her away with nowhere to go, she would try again and succeed."

The women were quiet, all lost in their thoughts. Julie was right. And so was Delta. Jo had broken her own rule, but it was too late now. Not that she would've handled the situation differently. Jo was certain if she hadn't allowed Raylene to stay, the woman would've jumped off the bridge, and her death would haunt Jo for the rest of her life.

"I'll go talk to her." Jo swallowed her last bite of food, rinsed her plate off in the sink and wandered out onto the front porch.

She could barely make out the woman curled up on the far end of the swing, her arms locked around her knees and staring out into the dark night.

Duke joined Jo on the porch, and they made their way to the swing. "Do you mind if I sit?" She didn't wait for a reply as she eased onto the other end.

The pup pawed at Raylene's leg and then leaped onto the swing, sandwiching himself between the women.

"I'm sorry we dragged up all of the painful memories."

There was a long moment of silence before Raylene spoke. "You didn't drag them up. They're there all the time, every waking minute I see Brock's face. I still remember the gunshot and running for

105

my life." She shifted slightly. "Do you know what I did?"

"No." Jo shook her head.

"I ran. I ran to save my own hide. I left Brock all alone to die. When I got back to the car, I called the cops. Do you have any idea how long I sat in the car waiting for the police, knowing my best friend was dead and I was responsible?"

"It must've been agonizing," Jo whispered.

"It was." Raylene released her grip on her knees and jabbed a finger at her chest. "It should've been me! I should've died, not Brock."

"But you didn't. God had other plans. You may not understand it today. Maybe you never will, as long as you're on this earth, but you must trust Him."

"God," Raylene scoffed. "God sure dealt me a crappy hand."

Jo nudged the porch floor with her foot and the trio began rocking back and forth. A silence settled between them, the only sound was of the crickets and an occasional bellow of a nearby bullfrog.

"This is your second chance, Raylene. You can take it or you can harbor anger and hatred and live the rest of your life being bitter."

"We'll see. Soon, you won't have to worry about me. I'll be long gone."

Jo couldn't argue the point. She thought of the women's comments after Raylene dashed out, how Jo had broken her own rules. She was in a pickle.

Duke let out a low grunt as he shifted to a more comfortable position.

Jo absentmindedly stroked his fur. "What was this business you and your friend were involved in that was so dangerous he was murdered?"

Raylene slowly lifted her head. "I'm not sure you'll like my answer."

# Chapter 8

Jo said the first thing that came to mind. "Were you a hired assassin?"

"Close. We were bounty hunters."

"You're kidding."

"Nope. Brock and I owned *Bay Hill Bail Agents* based out of Florida."

"How did you..."

Raylene finished Jo's question. "End up in a Kansas prison? We were working on a big job. We followed our jumper, that's what we called the ones who jumped bail, all the way from South Florida to Kansas."

"Wow." Jo let out a low whistle. "A bounty hunter."

"In Florida, the technical term is bond agent. In Kansas, it's better known as a bounty hunter. It was a lucrative business. For a while, Brock and I were making money hand over fist. There are a lot of criminals in Florida."

"There are a lot of criminals everywhere," Jo pointed out.

"True."

"So you set up some sort of sting. It backfired and your friend, who was also your partner, was murdered."

"And the corrupt judge, who also happened to be a person of interest, made sure the jury convicted me."

Some of the pieces were beginning to fall into place: Raylene's inquisitive nature, her finding the hoe under the hedge.

The screen door creaked open, and Delta emerged. "We were beginning to worry about you two."

"We're fine."

Raylene sprang to her feet. "I was about to call it a day. I'm whupped. Tomorrow is going to be a long day."

"I'll get the key to your unit, plus a key to the bathroom cabinet," Jo said.

Raylene told her which empty bathroom cabinet she planned to use.

"Did you give Raylene her bag of toiletries?" Delta asked.

"No. I forgot." Jo led the way inside. The other women were long gone, the dining room table cleared and the kitchen clean as a whistle.

Delta pulled a plastic bag from the coat closet and handed it to Raylene. "Inside are bottles of shampoo and conditioner, some disposable razors, body wash, hand soap, a toothbrush and a tube of toothpaste."

"Thank you. You all are too kind, too generous. I don't know how I can ever repay you for taking me in," Raylene said gratefully.

Jo, who had gone to her office to grab the keys, joined them. "Now don't forget to lock up the medicine cabinet after you put your stuff inside."

"Someone would steal a bottle of shampoo?" Raylene asked.

Delta and Jo exchanged a quick glance. "Unfortunately, there was a minor misunderstanding between a couple of the women. Someone's razors came up missing, and there was some finger pointing."

"Minor misunderstanding," Delta snorted. "We wrote Julie and Kelli up with a warning. It was tense for a few days. Just keep your stuff locked up, and there shouldn't be a problem."

"Will do," Raylene promised. "I'll see you back here for breakfast at seven sharp?"

"Yes," Delta nodded. "Be here or be hungry until lunchtime. It will be a light meal since Jo and I are heading to town for breakfast."

"Yes, ma'am." Raylene gave Delta a thumbs up before exiting through the back door.

Jo waited until she was gone. "Ten bucks says you'll never guess what line of business Raylene was in before being sent to prison."

"A corrections officer."

"No, but you're closer than I thought. She was a bond agent in Florida, also known as a bounty hunter."

Delta covered her mouth to stifle a yawn. "Her story is getting more complicated by the minute."

"Right? I say it's time to hit the hay. Tomorrow is shaping up to be a very busy day."

*****

Strong storms passed through sometime during the night, waking Jo from a sound sleep, and she had trouble falling back asleep. She spent hours worrying about Gary and his attack, how someone was targeting the farm.

Last, but not least, she wondered what would happen to Raylene if Pastor Murphy wasn't able to find a place for her to go.

The fact two of the other women pointed out Jo was breaking her own rules was cause for concern. She prayed it wouldn't create friction between the women.

Jo briefly considered moving Raylene into the main house. She quickly dismissed it, thinking it would look as if she was showing even more favoritism toward the woman, which was the last thing Jo wanted.

No, Raylene would have to go. There was no way around it. In the meantime, she was both looking forward to - and dreading the trip to town.

Other than making quick stops at the post office and an occasional stop for gas when Nash wasn't around, she wasn't familiar with the small town.

She hoped a visit might help her get to know some of the residents. She knew one woman for sure was against her, Debbie Holcomb. Surely, the woman wouldn't go to all the trouble of not only vandalizing her property but also attacking poor Gary.

Finally, Jo drifted off to sleep, waking early when the alarm went off. After a quick shower, she slipped on a pair of shorts and a button down blouse. She wet her hands and ran them through her hair, spiking her short locks in a semi-presentable look.

She slipped on a pair of sandals and then traipsed down the stairs.

Delta bustled back and forth across the kitchen; the tantalizing aroma of sizzling bacon filled the room.

Jo sniffed appreciatively. "It smells delicious in here. I thought you were making a light breakfast since we plan to eat in town."

Delta shot her a quick glance, never slowing as she darted to the fridge. "The women still gotta eat. Plus, I'm feeling a little guilty about us indulging in a fancy meal while they eat here."

"Your food is just as good, if not better than any paid meal."

"I like to think so." Delta handed Jo a pitcher of orange juice along with a plate of bagels and donuts. "I fried some bacon and scrambled a few eggs."

At seven sharp, the women gathered in the dining room. Nash was the last to arrive, and he took his place next to Jo.

While the others ate, Jo sipped her coffee and listened in. Thankfully, she didn't detect an underlying resentment toward the newcomer.

Raylene was subdued and only spoke when asked a direct question, which concerned Jo. Perhaps dredging up the painful memories of her partner's death was weighing heavy on her mind and making her sad.

Breakfast ended, with Delta reminding the women to check the bulletin board since the schedule had changed in Gary's absence.

Nash lingered behind. "Would you like me to head back to the hospital to check on Gary?"

"No." Jo thanked him. "I appreciate the offer. Delta and I are driving to town to run some errands. We'll swing by the hospital to check on him after we're done."

"Let me know if you change your mind." Nash gave her arm a gentle squeeze, and then he headed out.

"Oh boy," Delta batted her eyes. "He's got it bad."

"Got what bad?"

"You."

"What about me?"

"Nash...the way he looks at you. He gets all googly-eyed."

Jo could feel her cheeks warm. "That's crazy. Nash is not interested in me."

"Oh?" Delta lifted a brow.

"He's being nice, besides I'm his boss."

"Uh-huh." Delta glanced at her watch. "I'm going to run to my room to change. I'll meet you outside in fifteen."

"Perfect." Jo headed to her own bathroom to freshen up. She inspected herself in the bathroom mirror and scowled at her laugh lines, making them even more prominent. She remembered Delta's offhanded remark about Nash.

Jo's handyman was not interested in her. They were friends, nothing more.

"Jo Pepperdine, you look every day of your forty-nine long years." Jo had married once, many moons ago. It hadn't worked out and after a few short years of marital "un-bliss," the couple amicably parted ways.

That was back in the day when she lived in New York City. It was a different life back then, and one she didn't miss, not even a little. The middle of nowhere in Kansas was much more to Jo's liking.

She licked the tip of her finger and smoothed a wayward strand of hair before squaring her shoulders. "You must turn on the charm, Jo Pepperdine. You've been hiding from the world for too long, and it's high time to face it head on."

Delta was already waiting for Jo on the front porch. She shook the car keys. "I figured you would want to drive to town in style. You left the keys on your desk, not on the hook."

"I did? I must be losing it, which is probably why I let you talk me into having breakfast in town." Jo motioned to the door. "Let's go before I change my mind."

The closer they got to Divine, the more nervous Jo became. Some of these people had already passed judgment without ever meeting her or any of the women who lived in the halfway house.

Delta glanced over, reading Jo's mind. "It will be okay. They're either gonna like you or they're not. Some of 'em are gonna give you a chance and some of them never will."

"True." Jo glanced out the window at the farm fields. "Marlee seemed to think this was a good idea."

"And I think it's a good idea too. We're here." Delta swung the SUV into an empty parking spot, directly in front of Marlee's restaurant, *Divine Delicatessen.*

Jo gazed through the large glass window. The deli was busy, busier than she'd anticipated. "The place is busy."

"It's one of the only places in town that serves food, not counting the bar or the ice cream shop."

Delta shut the engine off and reached for the door handle. "You look like you're on your way to the executioner."

"I might as well be." Jo swallowed hard. "Let's get this over with."

# Chapter 9

Delta grabbed her friend's arm and led her inside the restaurant, where the smell of strong black coffee mingled with fried foods greeted them.

"I see a table over there." Jo began walking toward a small table, tucked away in the back corner.

"I like this one better." Delta plopped down at a table for four near the front.

"Fine." Jo frowned as she dropped her purse on an empty chair.

"Good morning." A server cheerily greeted the women, carrying a pot of coffee. "Will it be just the two of you?"

"Yes," Delta nodded.

"Coffee?"

"Please." Jo turned her cup over.

"Me, too," Delta watched the woman pour her coffee. "What are today's breakfast specials?"

"They're posted on the chalkboard near the door. Today's special is two eggs, bacon, a small stack of pancakes and toast, all for four dollars and ninety-nine cents."

"That's a decent deal. I'll take it," Delta said.

"Is it the quickest meal on the menu?" Jo asked. "We're kind of in a hurry."

"No. No, we're not." Delta rolled her eyes. "We're not in a hurry."

"Speak for yourself. Fine...we're not in a hurry, although I can think of a million things to do at home. I'll have the special," Jo said. "Eggs over easy, wheat toast."

"Ditto," Delta added. "Is Marlee around?"

"Yes." The woman nodded. "She's in the back."

"If you get a chance, could you tell her that Jo and Delta are here and we said 'hi'?"

"Of course." The woman jotted their order on a notepad and walked away.

Delta leaned across the table. "You need to get a grip on your semi anti-social behavior."

"I'm social enough. I live with all of you, plus I spend plenty of time surrounded by people when I'm working in the bakeshop and mercantile."

Marlee emerged from the back and hurried across the dining room. "Jo, I'm so glad you're here." She patted Jo on the shoulder and smiled at Delta. "The scowl on your face tells me Delta was the one behind this trip."

"Something like that," Jo muttered.

"I heard about poor Gary's incident. He's still in the hospital?"

"Yes. After we leave here, we're going to drive over there to check on him." Jo sipped her coffee.

"We thought you might know what people in town are saying about the incident."

Marlee shifted her feet. "People are saying you're harboring criminals. That's the reason you won't come to town."

"See?" Jo wagged her finger at Delta. "I knew it. They think we're some sort of colony of criminals, which makes absolutely zero sense."

"I set them straight every chance I get," Marlee said. "Debbie Holcomb is one of the residents spreading the rumor. The woman has it in for you."

"I-I've never even met her," Jo sputtered.

"But you did buy the old McDougall place at auction."

"What has that got to do with anything?"

Marlee lifted a brow. "You don't know?"

"Know what?" Jo shook her head.

"The owners died, leaving the estate in limbo. After the McDougalls' deaths, the siblings hired their own attorneys and sued each other."

Delta snapped her fingers. "Marlee, you're right. I forgot all about the family feud."

"What does this have to do with Debbie Holcomb?" Jo asked.

"She's a sibling," Delta said. "Debbie McDougall Holcomb."

"So she thinks I'm responsible for her losing the family farm? That's ridiculous. It went to auction. I bought it fair and square."

"Lawfully - yes," Marlee said. "According to the McDougalls, it's not as cut and dried."

"So they hired lawyers and lost it?" Jo lifted her coffee cup.

"Yes." Marlee explained how the long and protracted battle between the siblings and their attorneys left each of them deeply in debt. They couldn't afford to pay the attorneys' fees and ended up having to auction the place off. "Two of the siblings left town. The other two are still here, and Holcomb is one of them."

"Who...is the other?" Jo asked.

"Jesse McDougall," Marlee and Delta said in unison.

"Have I met him?"

"He's the postmaster." Delta's eyes grew wide. "Jo, the first incident, when your mailbox was destroyed. Is it possible that McDougall is behind the vandalism?"

"He doesn't run the mail routes. His nephew does, although he's been laid up with an injury for the last few weeks."

"Which fits in perfectly with the timeline of the vandalism," Jo said. "Or maybe it's Debbie Holcomb."

The women's food arrived, and Marlee excused herself. "I better get back to work. I'm glad you ladies came by. You need to stop in here more often."

"We'll see about that," Jo muttered. "I stay pretty busy at home."

Delta ignored Jo's grumblings. "We will," she promised.

While the women ate, they discussed Debbie Holcomb and Jesse McDougall, throwing out scenarios of how one or the other snuck onto the property.

"If you think about it, not only are they both familiar with the layout of the house, but also the buildings and the property," Delta said. "I wonder if Deputy Franklin has considered these two as possible suspects."

"The authorities would rather blame it on one of our residents," Jo pointed out. "I doubt they want to question one of their own."

The women finished their food; both agreeing that Marlee's breakfast was delicious and Jo insisting Delta's meals were every bit as good.

Marlee stopped by their table, as they were getting ready to leave. "I figured Debbie would be by this morning. She's usually in here toward the end of the week collecting expired baked goods for her church. I've got a whole bag full."

"She lives nearby?" Delta asked.

"Oh yes. If you go left out of here and to the stop sign, turn left again. Debbie's house is at the end of the street. You can't miss it. She has a huge 'No Trespassing' sign stapled to her tree out front."

"We'll deliver the baked goods," Delta said.

"We will?" Jo gasped. "The woman hates me. You heard Marlee. She has a huge 'No Trespassing' sign out front. She'll probably shoot us first and ask questions later."

"You would be doing me a huge favor if you could drop them off." Marlee waved dismissively. "Her bark is worse than her bite. Speaking of which, ignore the 'Beware of Dog' sign. She doesn't have a dog."

"I dunno about this," Jo shook her head. "I'm getting a bad feeling. This woman hates me."

"She doesn't know you," Delta argued.

"Debbie isn't a bad person, just a tad judgmental," Marlee said. "Although the fact you were the one who purchased her family property right under her nose probably didn't score you any brownie points."

"See?" Jo said. "This is a terrible idea."

"On the one hand, there's a chance she'll kick us off her property. On the other, if she is responsible, she'll know we're onto her and will think twice before trying something again," Delta said. "Besides, it's broad daylight. What could possibly happen?"

"I'll leave it up to you," Marlee said. "I would feel awful if I sent you over there and Debbie called the cops."

"Cops?" Jo said. "I see an arrest in my future."

"No way," Delta shook her head. "You're overreacting."

Despite Jo's reservations, Delta finally convinced her friend to swing by the woman's place to drop off the baked goods. The only thing swaying her decision was Delta's argument if the woman thought they were onto her, she might stop the attacks.

"Fine. We'll go, but be ready to run," Jo said.

"I think you could reason with her. You won't know unless you try. I'll go get the food." Marlee darted to the back, returning moments later carrying two large bags. "I had more baked goods than I thought. Thank you for delivering them."

"You're welcome." Delta grabbed the bags.

"Let me know how it goes." Marlee followed them to the exit. "Good luck."

The women climbed into the car and Delta backed onto the street.

"We're really gonna do this," Jo said. "If she shoots us, don't say I didn't warn you."

"She's not going to shoot us."

Delta crept to the corner and turned left. She drove to the end of the street and a tidy single story ranch home. Faded black and white striped awnings covered the front windows.

"Don't pull in the drive." Jo pointed to the large "No Trespassing" sign. "Marlee wasn't kidding."

"I have to agree, she does seem determined to keep people away."

"Which means us. Have you given any thought as to how we're going to charm her into liking us?"

"We have food." Delta reached in the back seat and grabbed the bags of baked goods. "At the very least we tried, right?"

"I guess," Jo sighed. "Let's do this before I change my mind." She reached for the door handle. "Do you see a pattern here? You're forcing me to do things outside of my comfort zone."

"It's good for you." Delta hopped out of the SUV.

Jo reluctantly trudged behind her; certain at any moment the woman would shoot them dead, right there in the driveway.

Delta waited for Jo to join her on the front step before pressing the doorbell. The chime echoed inside the house.

No one answered. Delta pressed it a second time. There was still no answer. "I guess she's not home. We might as well leave the stuff here." She set it on the stoop before changing her mind. "On second thought, I think I'll hang the bags on the garage door. That way, she can't miss them when she gets home."

"Then I say we hightail it out of here." The hair on the back of Jo's neck stood. She had the eerie feeling they were being watched and a sneaking suspicion the homeowner, Debbie, was behind the curtains, watching their every move. "This place gives me the creeps."

Delta finished hanging the second bag on the door handle when the crunch of tires on gravel, followed by a car's engine revving directly behind her caught her attention.

It was a sedan, speeding down the long drive, and straight toward them.

Jo shoved Delta out of the car's path. The vehicle came to a screeching halt, mere inches from where the women had just been standing.

# Chapter 10

The angry woman behind the wheel flung the door open and jumped out of the car. "You're trespassing."

"We came from *Divine Delicatessen* and are here to drop off some baked goods for Marlee." Jo pointed to the bags hanging on the doorknob.

"Marlee doesn't deliver."

"She did today." Delta met the woman's gaze. "We're helping her out, Debbie."

The woman ignored Delta and pinned Jo with a pointed stare. "Who are you?"

"I'm Joanna Pepperdine, the owner of *Second Chance Mercantile* and *Divine Baked Goods Shop* outside of town."

"You're the woman who is running an unlicensed bed and breakfast, but not for long."

"It isn't a bed and breakfast. It's a home for women and fully licensed under Kansas law," Jo said. "You can file complaints all day long, but you aren't going to shut me down."

"You're bringing the criminal element to our area," the woman replied. "Look at what happened to poor Gary Stein."

"None of the women residing on my property had anything to do with Mr. Stein's incident. In fact, we suspect the culprit is living right here in Divine." Jo jabbed her finger in Holcomb's direction. "And quite possibly standing right here in front of me."

The woman's eyes widened. "Are you accusing me of attacking Gary?"

"You're the only one who is determined to shut us down," Delta said. "Why not you?"

"That's the most absurd accusation I've ever heard." Holcomb fumbled inside her purse. "I'm going to call the police and report you for trespassing, for trying to break into my house and for threatening me."

"We haven't threatened you." Jo turned to Delta. "C'mon. Let's go. Ms. Holcomb obviously isn't in the mood to listen to reason. If you reach the sheriff's department, send them out my way. I'm going to suggest they investigate you as a potential suspect."

"You won't get away with threatening Debbie Holcomb! That farm is cursed. I hope it burns to the ground!"

Jo marched to the end of the drive. She climbed into the SUV and slammed the door shut. Delta hurried to the driver's side.

The woman, her face twisted in a mask of fury, ran to the end of the driveway.

"We better get out of here." Delta started the vehicle. She pressed on the gas, a little too hard. A spray of gravel pelted the "No Trespassing" sign. "Can you believe that?"

"She probably put a curse on the place," Jo said grimly. "Our name is going to be mud all over this town. I wouldn't put it past her to make good on her threat and try to burn my farm to the ground with us in it."

"Nah. She's nothing but a bag of hot air." Delta steered the SUV back onto the main street and parked in front of a small shop, *Claire's Collectibles and Antiques*. Next door to the antique shop was *Claire's Coin Laundromat*.

Colored twinkling lights beckoned them inside. "How cute is this place? I didn't notice it earlier." Jo stared through the windshield. "I wonder how a business in a small town like Divine manages to keep its doors open."

"The same way the mercantile and bakeshop stay in business. It's all of the tourists passing through on their way to the center of nowhere." It was Delta's favorite joke, how people drove to the middle of the country to see nothing.

Well, not absolutely nothing. The center point of the lower forty-eight states sported a small church, a couple of signs and rolling farm fields for as far as the eye could see. If not for the star attraction, the bakery and mercantile wouldn't exist, and neither would the halfway house.

"Claire owns this place, plus the coin laundromat next door. I figured you could meet her and check out her cool antiques." Delta held the door, and Jo stepped inside the small shop, the fragrant aroma of pine greeted them. Christmas music played softly in the background.

The shop was crammed from floor to ceiling. Jo couldn't decide where to look first. There were whimsical Santas, dressed in bright red suits and shiny black boots. Next to the display of Santas were several whimsical merry-go-rounds.

Tucked away in the corner was a curio cabinet, similar to the one in Jo's mercantile. It was filled with Hummel figurines. Jo recognized a couple -

one was the *Merry Wanderer* and the other, *Adventure Bound.*

"You like the Hummels?" A petite woman with inquisitive blue eyes and a beehive hairdo joined them.

Jo smiled when she realized she recognized the woman. She was a frequent visitor to the bakeshop and mercantile. "Mrs. Harcourt."

"Claire. You can call me Claire. I see you've finally found your way into town."

"We ate breakfast over at Marlee's place. Delta thought I might like to stop here to check out your shop. You have a nice collection of Hummels and a lot of angels."

"They're the Divine angels," Claire joked. "Aren't they lovely?" Her tone sobered. "I'm sorry to learn about Gary Stein's accident. I hear he's going to be okay."

"Yes. Thank God," Jo said. "We were going to visit him at the hospital on our way into town, but the nurses recommended we wait until after the doctor had a chance to see him first. We're heading there after we leave here."

"We don't believe Gary's injuries were an accident. We think someone attacked him, right after they tried to break into the mercantile," Delta said. "We were hoping to talk to a few of the residents to see what they're saying."

Claire adjusted a beaded tassel on a Victorian lamp and nodded. "I see. Well, it depends on whom you ask. Some say one of the residents at your place attacked Gary. Others say it's a local who wants to scare you into leaving."

"Debbie Holcomb," Delta guessed.

"Yes. She has it set in her mind you're bringing crime to Divine and sees it as her civic duty to get rid of you." Claire tilted her head. "Or it could be the fact you purchased the McDougall family estate, and she's still a little testy."

"I bought the home and property at an auction. If not me, someone else would've purchased it. The women at my place would never hurt Gary. He's like one of the family," Jo argued. "What do you think?"

"I think there's a great need for places like yours. That's why I make a point of shopping there on a regular basis, to show my support in small ways," Claire said. "Besides, Debbie doesn't have a leg to stand on. You're not breaking any laws, and there's not much she can do but huff and puff."

"And almost run us over," Delta muttered.

"Run you over?" Claire's eyes grew wide.

"It's a long story. We tried to reason with her," Jo explained. "It backfired, and she pretty much chased us off her property."

"She doesn't like people dropping by. You didn't notice her 'No Trespassing' signs?"

Jo shot Delta a triumphant look. "See?" She turned to Claire. "Who else in town is opposed to my housing the women?"

"There's crabby old Jesse McDougall who runs the post office, one of Debbie's siblings and another bitter family member. Unfortunately, he likes to go on about how you're ruining our quaint little town and lowering our property values." Claire waved dismissively. "Most folks ignore him. There are not many people in town he does like."

Jo thought about her damaged mailbox and post, how it was the first incident of trouble at her place. "He wouldn't happen to run the mail routes, too?"

"Nope. Jesse's nephew runs the rural routes 'round here. He's been out of commission for a couple of weeks now. Fell out of a tree stand he was building. Nice kid."

The phone rang, and Claire excused herself.

A display of antique silverware caught Delta's eye while Jo wandered up and down the aisles perusing Claire's collectibles. She found a Tiffany-style Victorian table lamp that would fit perfectly on the table in front of the living room window.

Claire finished her call and joined Jo. "That lamp is a fine piece."

"Yes, I do believe I have a perfect spot for it in my living room." Jo paid for her purchase. "Thank you for supporting my businesses."

"And you mine," Claire winked. "We troublemakers need to stick together."

Delta and Jo said their good-byes and stepped onto the sidewalk.

"What a neat little shop," Jo said. "I never realized Claire owned businesses in town. She's a nice lady."

"See?" Delta asked. "There are some decent people in this town, good and decent people."

"You're right, except for Debbie Holcomb," Jo said. "The verdict is still out on Jesse, who runs the post office. I remember him waiting on me a couple of times, but he never struck me as rude. Perhaps he didn't know who I was."

Delta snorted. "In this small town? Believe me, everyone knows everyone within a fifty mile radius." She glanced down the street. "Let's put the lamp in the SUV and then make a quick stop at the post office. We can always use some extra stamps."

After dropping off the lamp, the women strolled along the sidewalk; smiling at those they passed by. Jo started to relax when she realized people weren't staring at her. They passed several vacant buildings, their windows boarded up.

Jo's anxiety returned when they reached the entrance to the post office. "You sure you're up for another confrontation?"

"We're already here. It can't hurt to have a look around, maybe get a feel for the postmaster's attitude." Delta reached for the door handle. "Remember, he has motive for wanting you out of town, not to mention opportunity."

"True." Jo eyed the door warily. "What if he tries to attack us like his sister, Debbie, did?"

"He's not going to attack us." Delta wrinkled her nose. "He's a federal employee, and held to a higher standard."

"Like that means anything. Remember the phrase 'going postal?'"

"He's not going to do anything." Delta marched inside the building, and Jo reluctantly followed behind.

There were two people in line while another woman stood off to the side, near the mailboxes.

Delta and Jo joined the line. When they reached the front, the gray-haired man peered at them over the rim of his glasses. "Afternoon."

"Good morning," Delta corrected. "I would like a book of stamps, please."

The man reached into a drawer, pulled out a book of stamps and slapped them on the counter. "That'll be nine dollars and eight cents."

Jo squeezed in next to Delta and placed her debit card on the counter. "You're the postmaster."

"I am." The man swiped her card and handed it back. "Sign on the screen."

Jo scribbled her signature. "Thank you. What a lovely post office you have."

Jesse lifted a brow. "You're joking. Will there be anything else?"

Jo's face grew warm, and before she could stop herself, she said the first thing that popped into her head. "Are you always this friendly?"

"I'm running a business, not a social get-together. Will there be anything else?" he repeated.

"You are a rude man," Delta fumed. "No wonder no one in this town likes you." She spun on her heel and strode out of the store. She didn't slow until she reached the parking lot.

Jo hurried after her. "Two for two. First Debbie Holcomb and now this rude man. I'm beginning to wonder if this is a prerequisite for living in Divine."

"They're related," Delta said. "We need to pray for them. They seem miserable."

"Miserable relatives. I'm beginning to understand why the siblings decided to hire separate attorneys and sue each other."

The women trudged across the street, passing by *Twisty Treat* ice cream shop.

Delta slowed to study the menu. "Ice cream sounds good."

"Dessert after breakfast?" Jo laughed.

"Ice cream is mostly milk." Delta lowered her chin, peering down at the menu. "They also serve chilidogs, sub sandwiches and side salads."

The young woman behind the counter opened the order window. "Can I help you?"

"Yes, I'll take a value banana split with an extra side of hot fudge." Delta glanced behind her. "What do you want, Jo? My treat."

"I'll take a small vanilla cone dipped in chocolate."

"Coming right up." The woman made quick work of completing their orders and then handed them to Jo while Delta paid.

"I haven't eaten an ice cream cone in ages." Jo licked the sweet stream of vanilla that trailed down the side of her cone. "Thank you, Delta."

"You're welcome. This eases the pain of our morning run-ins." Delta shoved her wallet in her purse and reached for the banana split. "There's a small park next door. We can take a load off and enjoy the treats over there."

The women settled in on a park bench facing a center fountain and coin pool. A small jungle gym and a swing set were on the other side of the fountain.

"Well? Do you think Debbie Holcomb or Jesse McDougall could be responsible for the vandalism and Gary's attack?"

"I don't know what to think. The fact Holcomb came at us with her car and totally freaked out screams instability." Jo bit the tip of the chocolate swirl. "The postmaster is a rude man, but then again, if you think about it, the first incident was my smashed mailbox, and then the attempted break-in at the mercantile followed by Gary's attack."

"Not to mention Claire said the nephew, the route deliverer, has been laid up for a couple of weeks now. So maybe he is responsible. It fits into the timing of the first incident." Delta scooped up a large chunk of banana and dipped it in her container of hot fudge. "This is so good. We need to get out more often."

"Speaking of out, we need to head to the hospital to check on Gary. I assume you're done snooping around town," Jo teased.

"For now."

The women finished their sweet treats and returned to the SUV. During the drive to the hospital, they chatted about Raylene and the other women. Before Jo knew it, they were pulling into the hospital's parking lot.

After checking in at the reception desk, they took the elevator to the second floor and stopped by the nurse's station before making their way to Gary's room.

Jo rapped lightly, catching the attention of two nurses who were standing beside Gary's empty bed. "We're here to see Gary Stein. Has he been moved?"

"I...no, he hasn't been moved." One of the nurses hurried to the doorway. "Mr. Stein appears to be missing."

# Chapter 11

Delta's jaw dropped. "He's missing?"

"Mr. Stein was determined to leave the hospital this morning. I assured him the doctor would be around to examine him, but he apparently decided he didn't want to wait."

"Those are his clothes?" Jo pointed to the pile of clothes on the overbed table.

The nurse nodded. "Yes. If he left the hospital, he's still wearing his hospital gown."

"He couldn't have gone too far. He doesn't have a vehicle. As far as I know, he didn't even have a cell phone on him." Jo stepped back into the hall. "I'll take a look around downstairs."

Delta stayed behind to help the nurses search the second floor's public areas while Jo returned to the main floor. She circled the waiting area. There was no sign of Gary.

She stopped near the restrooms and then approached a man, sitting nearby. "I was wondering if you could do me a huge favor. My friend seems to be missing, and I thought he might be inside the men's restroom."

"Sure." The man dropped the magazine he was holding. "What does he look like?"

"His name is Gary. He's medium height, thin and balding on top," Jo said. "And he's wearing a hospital gown."

"I'll be right back."

Jo waited near the door while the man checked. He returned moments later, shaking his head. "The restroom is empty."

"Thank you for checking." Jo made a large loop around the hospital's main level, but there still no sign of Gary.

She stopped at the information desk adjacent to the main entrance. "Yes, I was wondering if you happened to see a balding man. He's medium height, thin and wearing a hospital gown."

Both desk clerks shook their heads "no."

Jo's concern was escalating to near panic. What if Gary was determined to leave, he made it out of the building before collapsing and was now lying somewhere unconscious?

She darted out the main doors and onto the sidewalk. If she were in Gary's shoes, what would she do? Surely, he wouldn't try to hitch a ride home clad only in a hospital gown.

Jo shaded her eyes and peered into the parking lot, but there was no sign of her friend. She turned to head back inside, hoping Delta and the nurses were able to track him down when she caught a glimpse of hospital blue, flapping in the wind near the bus stop bench.

A man who bore a striking resemblance to Gary was seated on the bench, his back to her. She jogged down the sidewalk. "Gary Stein!"

Gary turned when he heard his name. "Jo." He abruptly stood, the back flap of his gown catching a breeze and giving all in the vicinity a bird's eye view of his bare backside.

Jo looked away, but it was too late. She'd seen too much. She averted her gaze and approached the bench. "Gary, you cannot leave the hospital. Delta and the nurses are upstairs, tearing the place apart looking for you."

"I got sick and tired of waiting. The nurses refused to give me back my clothes, so I left." Gary clutched the back of the open gown. "I told 'em I was leaving, clothes or not."

"How...did you plan on getting home?"

"Nash called my room a little while ago. He said you were on the way and would be here before

154

noon. I figured I would see you pull in, but I missed the truck."

"Delta and I drove the Range Rover." Jo placed a light hand on his arm, propelling him toward the hospital entrance. "You need to let the doctor take a look at you before we drive you home."

"I'm not going back in there." Gary stubbornly shook his head. "They've been poking and prodding me, giving me a worse headache than I had when I got here."

"But you suffered a serious injury. We need to make sure you're all right. Surely, you don't want to leave if you shouldn't."

Gary's hand trembled as he adjusted his glasses. "Well. He said he was going to let me go home until he found out there was no one to keep an eye on me."

"So the doctor said you could go home if someone was there?" Jo asked.

"Yep. Last night before he left."

"I have an idea." Jo slipped her arm through his and gently led him toward the entrance. "In fact, I'm sorry I didn't think of this earlier. I think you should come back to my place. Delta, Nash and I will be on hand to keep an eye on you. I have plenty of room."

"Are you sure?" Gary stopped. "I don't want to be any trouble."

"You're no trouble at all," Jo said firmly. "In fact, I insist. Let's get back to your room and talk to the doctor. If he's okay with it, we'll grab your things and take you home."

*****

On the way back to the farm, Delta swung by Gary's place, so he could pack some clean clothes and check on things.

Delta waited in the SUV while Jo kept a watchful eye on him as he gathered his belongings. He was moving at a snail's pace, and she could tell he was tiring, but he refused to stop and rest.

His complexion had paled considerably, and when they reached the house, Jo insisted he go right to bed. Delta took over, mothering Gary and insisting he needed some decent food and then plenty of rest.

With her houseguest in Delta's capable hands, Jo began making her rounds, checking on the staff. She started in the bakeshop and then crossed over to the mercantile where Sherry was training Raylene.

She stopped by the workshop to fill Nash in on the recent developments and told him the story of how she found Gary on the bus stop bench, naked except for the flimsy hospital gown.

"That sounds about right," Nash chuckled. "Gary is stubborn as a mule." His expression sobered. "I'm glad you invited him to stay here, Jo. You have a good heart."

Jo's pulse ticked up a notch when their eyes met. "Thanks, Nash. Sometimes I wonder." Jo thought of her sharp words with Debbie Holcomb and Jesse, the postmaster. Of course, the area locals were concerned about the halfway house residents.

If truth be told, and she was in their shoes, she would feel the same. But everyone deserved a second chance. The women had paid their dues, and now it was time to let them start over again.

She thought of her own life, and how she'd desperately needed a second chance, too.

"I heard there was a dust-up over in the common area. One of the women got in Raylene's face, and Sherry had to break it up."

"You're kidding. This is the first I've heard of a problem. I made my rounds, and no one said a peep."

"They got it settled." Nash reached for a sheet of sandpaper. "Raylene seems like a nice woman, but the others... Don't get me wrong, I think you did the right thing in letting Raylene stay. Standing on the outside, looking in, I guess the other women might view it a little differently."

"What do you mean?"

"I mean, you kind of bent the rules, just a little." Nash pinched his thumb and index finger together. "Raylene technically shouldn't have been allowed in, so my guess is there's a little jealousy. They think you're showing favoritism."

"I would never do that," Jo said. "I treat all of the women equally. Yes, I admit I did bend the rules, but only temporarily. As soon as Pastor Murphy is able to find somewhere for Raylene to go, she'll be on her way."

"Like I said, you got a big heart, Jo. The other women know it, too." The unspoken rest of Nash's sentence hung heavy in the air. He was right. Jo *had* bent the rules, but she couldn't throw Raylene out. The poor woman had nowhere to go.

"She jumped off *Divine Bridge*, you know that?"

"Yep. A divine intervention saved her life. Evan is telling everyone in town how he saw the two men on the shoreline near Raylene's body and when he got down there, they were gone. She shouldn't have lived, that's for sure."

There was a light rap on the door. Nash opened it to find Deputy Brian Franklin on the other side, hat in hand. "Sherry told me I might find you in here."

"Hello, Deputy Franklin," Jo greeted him. "You were on my list to call. Did you find anything on the garden hoe?"

"Yes, we did. It appears to be blood. You were right, and I'm sure the hoe was the weapon the person used to strike Gary Stein on the back of the head." The deputy stepped inside the workshop. "Before I came in here, I took the liberty of circling the property to see if I could find any other clues."

"Raylene and I also looked," Jo said. "We didn't see anything. I might have one more piece of information." She told him how Sherry mentioned hearing a *clunk* outside her window the previous morning around six-thirty. "She remembers because it woke her out of a sound sleep."

"It makes sense," Nash said. "Her room is near the back of the mercantile. If they also tried to break in the back, it would be near her apartment."

Jo involuntarily shivered at the thought of an intruder on her property and in close proximity to the women. "I'm beginning to wonder if I need to add a self-defense class."

"Might not be a bad idea." The deputy shifted uncomfortably. "Is Delta around?"

"Yes. She's in the house," Jo said. "Do you need to talk to her, too?"

"One of the Divine residents stopped by the sheriff's department a short time ago. She claims you and Delta, well...that you were trespassing on her property."

"Debbie Holcomb?"

"Yes, ma'am. She claims you were trying to break into her garage and she caught you. When she got out of the car and asked you what you were doing, you threatened her."

"Th-that's absurd," Jo sputtered. "Delta can corroborate our story. We did no such thing. You can ask Delta yourself."

Jo flung the workshop door open and marched across the parking lot, up the steps and into the house, muttering under her breath.

The younger deputy traipsed after Jo, following her into the house and kitchen where they found Delta in front of the stove. She did a double take when she saw the deputy follow Jo in. "Now what happened?"

"You'll never guess who had the nerve to file a police report against us," Jo fumed.

"That witch Holcomb." Delta wiped her hands on her apron. "I'm not surprised. Ten bucks says she claims we not only trespassed but were trying to break into her garage."

"And we threatened her," Jo added.

"So you were on her property earlier today." The deputy reached into his pocket and pulled out a notepad.

"You're going to write this up?" Delta asked.

"I'm sorry, but I have to. Were you in Ms. Holcomb's garage?"

"Marlee, the owner of *Divine Delicatessen*, asked us to drop off some baked goods at Holcomb's place. Delta rang the doorbell. No one answered so we decided to hang the bags of food on the handle."

"And Ms. Holcomb happened to pull into the drive at the exact moment you were leaving the baked goods." The deputy plucked a pen from his pocket and began scribbling furiously.

"Yes. I was placing the bags on the door, which wasn't latched. It started to swing open, which is when the nasty woman showed up," Delta said. "We were certainly not trying to break into her house."

Deputy Franklin glanced up. "She also claims you threatened her."

"She gave us the middle finger and chased us to the end of the drive," Jo said.

"I returned the gesture and took off, although I may have pressed on the gas pedal a tad too hard and threw a few rocks," Delta said.

"Is that all?"

"Yes," Delta and Jo answered in unison.

"I appreciate your time. I'll file the report, and this should be the end of it." The deputy flipped the notepad shut and shoved it in his pocket. "Just a little friendly advice...I would avoid Ms. Holcomb's property. She's not too keen on visitors if you know what I mean."

"You can be sure we will never set foot on her property again," Jo promised.

"Good. I'll be on my way. I want to stop by Mr. Stein's place to ask him a few questions about his attack."

"He's staying with us. He's upstairs resting," Delta said. "The conk on the head affected him more than he's letting on. If you can put off questioning until tomorrow, I think he'll be feeling better."

"I understand. It can wait until tomorrow." The deputy placed his hat atop his head. "I would like to stop by the mercantile to chat with Sherry before I go."

Jo thanked the deputy for the update and led him back to the store. She returned to the workshop, knocking lightly before stepping inside.

Nash met her at the door. "What happened?"

Jo gave him a brief rundown of the run-in with Debbie Holcomb. "We hoped to clear the air with Holcomb, but our visit had the exact opposite effect." She changed the subject. "Going back to the incident earlier with the women, I guess I better have a chat with them during dinner this evening to try to clear the air."

In the meantime, Jo was up for one of her more daunting tasks. "It's time to take Julie for a drive."

"You sure you're ready for that?" Nash grinned.

"I'm never ready." Jo patted the top of her head. "I swear I get most of my gray hairs from the drives."

Jo was determined to make sure the women were taught all of the basic skills needed to re-enter society, and one of the most important was independence. This included the knowledge of not only opening bank accounts, balancing a checkbook, operating a computer and filling out a job application, but also driving.

Some of the women breezed through a driving refresher course while others...not so much. Julie was a new resident, so Jo hadn't had an opportunity to test her driving skills.

When Jo mentioned it the other day, Julie's complexion paled, and she gave Jo a deer-in-the-headlights look. She suspected Julie might need a little extra practice judging by her reaction.

"Do you mind if I take the truck?"

"Be my guest." Nash grabbed a set of keys off the hook and handed them to Jo. "You sure you don't want me to handle the driving?"

"No. I would feel terrible if you got in an accident. It's up to me to handle this." She thanked Nash for the keys and exited the workshop to track down Julie. She found her in the kitchen with Delta.

Jo stepped inside, dangling the keys in front of her. "It's drive time," she sing-songed.

"Oh no." Julie swallowed hard. "I...I think I already mentioned I'm not a good driver, and I get even more nervous when there's someone in the car. Besides, I plan on moving to the city and taking public transportation."

"That's all fine and dandy, but you should at least have some basic driving skills in the event of an emergency," Jo said. "Today will be a piece of cake. I promise."

Julie cast Delta a helpless glance.

"You'll be fine with Miss Jo." Delta patted Julie's shoulder. "All you gotta do is listen to what she says, stay calm and before you know it?" Delta snapped her fingers. "You'll be begging Jo to drive her around."

"I doubt it," Julie muttered. "I feel like throwing up."

Jo placed a light hand on Julie's back, propelling her out of the kitchen. "Daylight is burning."

During the walk from the house to the truck, Julie tried desperately to convince Jo she wasn't up for a drive.

Jo had been through this before. Some of the women were deathly afraid of getting behind the wheel. Unless they conquered their fears, driving was one more obstacle in an already crowded path to independence.

While Jo climbed behind the wheel, Julie circled to the other side and climbed in the passenger seat.

After Julie was seated, Jo started the truck and then briefly explained the important moving parts.

When Jo first started the driving refresher course, she didn't bother explaining the mechanics, until she found one of the women had never driven a car. Now, she never assumed anything and started from ground zero.

Jo shifted the truck into drive, and they coasted in circles around the parking lot. Finally, she drove the truck behind the workshop and onto the two-lane path that ran along the fence line, leading to the gardens and beehives out back.

As soon as they were on the two-lane path, Jo shifted into park and climbed out. "It's time to switch."

"Are you sure? I think I need to observe a little longer."

"No. The sooner you get behind the wheel, the sooner you'll conquer your fear," Jo motioned her to come around. "Come on."

Julie reluctantly slid out of the truck and trudged to the driver's side. She slid onto the seat and pulled the door shut while Jo took her place in the seat Julie vacated. "Seatbelts first."

Jo snapped her seatbelt and Julie followed suit.

"Now. Put your foot on the brake, the pedal to the left."

Julie glanced down at the floorboard and shifted her foot.

"Press down gently and keep it down."

Julie nodded. "Okay."

"Now shift the lever until you see it's on the 'D' on the center console."

Julie gingerly shifted into drive.

"Slowly take your foot off the brake."

The truck crept along the rutted path. All the while, Jo encouraged the woman in a calm and soothing voice. "You're doing great. See? You *can* do it."

Julie nodded, her eyes glued to the truck's windshield.

"You can give it a little gas. Just a little."

Julie pressed her foot on the gas pedal, and the truck lurched forward.

Jo's head jerked back. "A little smoother next time. If you stomp too hard, we'll end up with whiplash."

"Okay." The truck slowed and then picked up speed as Julie pressed on the pedal.

They reached the end of the dirt path.

"We're gonna turn left." Jo coaxed her through her first turn, and they crept along the back of Jo's property.

She looked down for a fraction of a second when Julie suddenly slammed on the brakes, causing Jo's head to whip back and smack the headrest.

"Whoa!"

Jo's head shot up. "What in the world?"

# Chapter 12

One of Jo's beehives lay on its side. Angry bees swarmed around it.

"Quick! Roll up the window!" Jo yelled.

Julie rolled the window up. "Now what?"

"We'll have to head back to the workshop and grab the beekeeper suit. Back up and turn around."

Julie shot her a look of sheer terror. "I..."

"Okay. Let's switch places." Jo unbuckled her seatbelt and crawled across the seat, climbing over Julie, who was sliding toward the spot Jo vacated.

Jo threw the truck in reverse and headed back toward the front of the farm.

"I wonder if someone knocked it over," Julie said.

"I was wondering the same thing. I know Gary said the platform needed some adjusting. It could be with last night's heavy rains, the ground softened causing the beehive to fall."

Jo drove as fast as she dared, jostling the women as they sped down the dirt path toward the front of the property. When she reached the outbuildings, she shifted into park and hopped out. "Stay here. I'll be right back."

She darted into the workshop. "Nash, we need some help." The loud buzz of the saws drowned out Jo's words.

"Nash!" Jo waved wildly.

Finally, Nash noticed Jo. He shut the saw off and removed his safety goggles. "Hey, Jo."

"I hate to bother you, Nash. Julie and I drove to the back of the property, to the beehives. One of them is on its side. The bees are swarming."

"I've been meaning to build a better platform. In fact, it was next on my list. I have Gary's suit in my workshop." Nash reached for the bee apron, hanging on a hook nearby. "I'll get down there right now and try to right it."

"We'll give you a lift," Jo said.

As soon as Nash donned the full beekeeper gear and climbed into the bed of the truck, Jo drove back to the overturned hive, parking a safe distance away.

Nash climbed out of the truck's bed. The angry bees swarmed him as he gently righted the hive. Several of the bees attacked his hood and veil.

"Nash is a brave man," Julie whispered.

"Yes, he is. I would've freaked out by now."

Nash checked the base of the hive and then checked the other hives before giving Jo a thumbs-up and climbing back into the bed of the truck.

Jo finished circling the property and eased the truck in front of the workshop. She climbed out and waited for Nash to join her. He had already removed the hood and veil, and Jo noticed a small welt beginning to form on the side of his neck.

"You got stung?"

"Yeah." Nash touched his neck. "One of the little buggers snuck in under a gap in the suit."

"We'll get the gap fixed pronto." Jo took the hood from Nash. "Delta is a whiz with a sewing machine." She thanked Nash for helping right the beehive.

After he left, Jo leaned in the cab of the truck. "It's time for us to switch places again."

"Do we have to?"

"Yes."

"I'm feeling kind of sick to my stomach." Julie clutched her gut. "Just the thought of driving makes me want to throw up."

"Then keep the window rolled down," Jo joked.

Julie's second attempt at driving went a little smoother than the first. When they passed by the beehives, the women rolled the windows up. They drove to the second, larger garden, where they stopped to inspect the vegetables before returning to the front.

"You did good." Jo took the keys from Julie. "I give you a B+ on driving."

"Thanks. I'm glad it's over." Julie headed to the store to relieve Sherry while Jo stopped to thank Nash and check on his sting.

"It's nothing a little baking soda and water can't fix." He nodded toward the door. "How did the driver's training go?"

"I think I gained a few more gray hairs, but I'm no worse for the wear," Jo joked.

"Listen, I was thinking about something," Nash said. "The farmer next door, Dave Kilwin, have you met him?"

"No."

"Well, when you mentioned the McDougalls owning the farm and how the siblings hired separate attorneys to sue each other, I got to thinking. Kilwin hired me to do a little repair work around his place, right before the auction. He was also hot to purchase this property."

"You don't say. So he may be another angry resident, upset with me for purchasing the property."

"And running successful businesses to boot," Nash said. "It's a thought."

"He would certainly have a reason for wanting me out. I'm sure he knows about the residents here. How well do you know him?"

"Like I said, he hired me to do some minor repairs. Can't say if he's bitter or angry. I know he was one of the people interested in purchasing your property."

"Do you mind showing me where he lives? I'm not sure I know which property is his," Jo said.

"Not at all." Nash followed Jo out of the shop and to the truck. They drove past Jo's place, to the first dirt road on the right.

Nash slowed the truck, weaving back and forth as he dodged the potholes. A large red barn along with a small, low-lying ranch appeared on the right. "That's his place."

Jo peered out the passenger window. "His property butts up to the side of mine."

"Yep. Check out his sign." Nash pointed to a sign, hanging on the front of a wooden wagon.

*Fresh produce and eggs for sale.*

"He's running a business," Jo said.

"Just like you, except yours is much larger."

"Maybe he wanted to purchase the property and expand his businesses," Jo theorized.

"It could very well be. I can't say as I suspect he's responsible for your vandalism and Gary's attack," Nash said.

"I'm not ruling anyone out." Jo tugged on her seatbelt. "Where does this road go?"

"It circles around the entire block and the back side of your property."

Nash sped up, and they drove to the end of the road. They made another turn. "Starting here, at the back of your property, and all along the other side is part of the *Kansas Creek Reservation*."

"American Indians?" Jo eyed the fields and tree line.

"Yes. Their property butts up to yours. They own thousands of acres."

"Interesting," Jo murmured.

Nash made a couple more turns and ended the trip where they began - in front of Jo's property.

"I'm adding more suspects by the minute. Right in my own backyard." Jo thanked Nash for taking her on the tour before making her way inside the house.

Delta was in the kitchen, peering into a large pot on the stove.

"Something smells delicious." Jo leaned over her shoulder and sniffed appreciatively, the smell of simmering vegetables and chicken causing her stomach grumble. "What are you making?"

"Chicken noodle soup." Delta glanced over her shoulder. "Where have you been hiding?"

"I took Julie for a drive, and then Nash and I took a spin around the block." Jo leaned her hip on the edge of the counter. "Did you know our neighbor down the road, David Kilwin, was also interested in purchasing this property?"

"No kidding. I've seen him around town, although I don't know him very well."

"Nash drove me by his place. His property backs up to ours. He has a sign out front, 'Fresh produce and eggs for sale.'"

"So he was hoping to buy this place and expand his business," Delta said. "Wouldn't take much for him to sneak across the property and destroy your mailbox or attack Gary."

"Yep, so now we have three potential suspects - Debbie Holcomb, her brother, Jesse McDougall, and our neighbor, David Kilwin. I also found out an Indian reservation backs up to my property."

"The *Kansas Creek Reservation*? I went there one time, many moons ago. They own a lot of land in the area." Delta grabbed a ladle from the drawer and returned to the stove. "I need a taste tester. Let me know if you think this tastes too salty." She dipped the ladle in the pot and then handed it to Jo.

Jo sampled the savory concoction. "It's perfect. What's the occasion?"

"I'm making this for Gary. He said he hasn't eaten a home-cooked meal since the last time he was here for dinner." Delta crossed her arms. "The poor man has been eating frozen dinners since Teresa died."

"So your plan is to fatten him up."

"Have you noticed how thin he's gotten?" Delta rambled on about keeping Gary there until she was sure he could take care of himself, and Jo wholeheartedly agreed. Not only was there plenty of room for Gary, but Delta loved taking care of others.

Jo excused herself to head to her small office, what had once been the keeping room. She was intrigued when she first heard the phrase and decided to do a little research. Keeping rooms were popular in colonial times. The heat from the kitchen kept the keeping room warm, making it one of the few heated areas of the house.

To Jo, it was one of the coziest spots in the house and a welcome retreat when she wanted to be alone. Along with an antique desk and weathered oak banker's chair, she placed a comfy overstuffed recliner, a small side table and reading lamp near the window. The reading nook overlooked the backyard and open fields.

She settled in behind the desk. Her first task was to check the business and personal bank accounts, and then Jo began sifting through her emails.

One of the emails was from her financial planner, updating her on some new investment opportunities. Jo couldn't make heads or tails of the information, whether the planner was telling her it was a good investment or to avoid it at all costs.

She trusted her planner implicitly, and Jo, an already wealthy woman, was even wealthier because of some smart moves the planner recommended.

Jo exited the emails and clicked on her investment portfolio. It still shocked her every time she checked the statement's bottom line and saw all of the zeros. It took many years for Jo to accept the fact that she had more money than she could ever spend.

It also took many years for her to come to grips with the guilt the wealth caused. The term *blood money* always came to Jo's mind, although it wasn't technically the case. It just felt that way.

Of course, she could use the money to expand the farm, but Jo wanted to prove to herself that the halfway house and businesses could succeed without her having to tap into her personal funds.

The only person, other than Jo's financial planner, who knew about the money and her past, was Delta. And the only reason Delta knew was because she'd accidentally opened a piece of Jo's mail, her investment portfolio.

She still remembered the day she'd wandered into the kitchen to check on Delta. It was right after Jo hired her and Delta moved in.

Delta sat at the kitchen table, an expression of disbelief on her face as she held a folded sheet of paper in her hand.

"Are you all right? You look like you've seen a ghost."

"No. I..." Delta held out the paper. "I'm sorry. I grabbed the mail and left yours on your desk. I thought this one was mine, so I opened it." She handed Jo the paper, lowering her eyes and avoiding her gaze. "I'm sorry."

Jo glanced at the paper, a copy of her quarterly portfolio statement and her heart sank. "I suppose you're wondering about this."

"It's none of my business," Delta shook her head. "You don't have to explain anything."

Jo pulled out the kitchen chair and sat next to her friend. "I think I should." She poured out the whole sordid story of how she came into being a wealthy woman.

Delta listened quietly without interrupting a single time. After Jo finished, Delta popped out of the chair and hugged Jo as tears streamed down her cheeks.

Her friend knew it all now, and she still cared for her. "You can leave if you like and I wouldn't blame you." Jo swiped at her wet face.

"Honey, you ain't getting rid of me that easy," Delta declared. "Besides, you've got a skewed view

186

of this entire situation. You have nothing to blame yourself for, and even if you made a mistake? Well, shoot, we all make mistakes in life."

"I could've handled things differently," Jo whispered.

"Hindsight's 20/20. You can't keep looking in the rearview mirror, Jo. You gotta keep moving forward. Look at all of the good that's come out of tragedy."

"There has been some good." Jo hiccupped. "It's my motivator."

"And a good motivator, too. Now it's time we best get back to work."

"This is between us." Jo picked up the sheet of paper.

"Absolutely. I'll take this one to my grave," Delta promised.

The women never discussed Jo's massive wealth again and Delta, true to her promise, never breathed a word, at least as far as Jo knew.

Jo clicked out of the screen, finished sorting through her things and then headed back to the kitchen. Delta was nowhere in sight, but Jo could hear the floor creak overhead, and she suspected her friend was checking on Gary.

With all of her bookkeeping duties taken care of, it was time for Jo's weekly inspection of the women's apartment units, another of Jo's rules and something the women agreed to before moving in.

Jo wanted to trust each of the women, but it was something earned, not automatically given. "Trust, but verify," was a favorite quote. So far, she hadn't been disappointed.

The inspections were mandatory and unannounced. Jo switched up her weekly inspections. Sometimes, she worked her way from end to end. Other times, she started with the middle units while others she chose at random.

If the women were around, they had no idea where she was going to start. This time, her plan was to start with a middle unit and then ping-pong back and forth, working her way to the ends.

The first two units were a breeze, the rooms tidy and everything in place. Jo inspected the dressers' contents. She checked under the beds and in the small closets before moving to the next.

Emily's former unit, now Raylene's unit, was next in line. The room was as tidy as the others were. She inspected the contents of the four-drawer dresser first, before checking under the bed. She also tugged on the windowsill to make sure it was locked before pulling back the covers and inspecting the sheets and blankets.

Jo wasn't sure why she checked the bedding, other than she knew some incarcerated inmates used every available means to hide contraband...including drugs.

She smoothed the covers back in place and then wandered to the closet where she skimmed through the meager contents. Jo made a mental note to have Raylene take a closer look around the mercantile for more clothes.

A pair of worn tennis shoes and a cheap pair of dollar store flip-flops were on the closet floor. Jo's throat clogged as she gazed at the woman's meager worldly possessions.

It was moments like these Jo wanted to load all of the women up in the SUV, drive to the nearest mall and let them shop to their heart's content, but she knew she wouldn't be doing them any favors.

Soon, they would be on their own, in an unforgiving world who judged them even more harshly than their fellow inmates. So...she stuck to her rule of no unexpected and unearned clothes. The only exceptions were birthdays when Jo splurged a little.

She finished inspecting the contents of the closet before moving on to the nightstands. The drawers were empty. She shut the bottom drawer and turned to go when the tip of her shoe bumped into something hard, wedged under the bottom of the dresser.

Jo dropped to her knees for a closer look. There was definitely something tucked under the dresser. She stuck her hand underneath, pulled out the rectangular, metal object and stared at it in disbelief.

"What are you doing?"

# Chapter 13

Jo spun around, answering Raylene's question with one of her own. She flipped open the multi-purpose tool's sharp blade and held it up. "What is this?"

"What is that?" Raylene asked. "I've never seen it before in my life."

"I found it under the edge of the dresser."

"It must have belonged to the woman who moved out yesterday. Like I said, I've never seen this before in my life. There's no way it's mine. I've been here for little more than a day and haven't been anywhere to have gotten my hands on it."

The woman had a point. Unless she somehow managed to hide it in her pocket or shoe, she was certain Pastor Murphy would never have given a suicidal person a weapon, not to mention he knew

Jo's rules and that weapons were grounds for immediate expulsion.

On the other hand, it was in her apartment. Perhaps the tool belonged to Emily, and she dropped it under the nightstand. Jo immediately dismissed the thought. Emily would never have risked concealing a weapon.

"Maybe someone planted it in my room," Raylene said. "I don't think all of the women here are keen on me being here."

Jo sat on the edge of the bed, contemplating her new arrival and the trouble she was creating. "I heard you got into a minor incident with one of the other residents in the common area."

"Yep." Raylene joined her on the edge of the bed. "Seems there's a pecking order regarding the bathroom cabinets. I put my stuff in the one I picked out and was told in no uncertain terms I couldn't use it. I told them you gave me the key, so it was mine."

"Really?" Jo remembered a recent incident between Michelle and Julie, and an argument over their toiletries. "Was it Michelle or Julie?"

"Maybe." Raylene's shoulders slumped. "I don't want to throw anyone under the bus and would rather forget about it."

"I planned to discuss the incident at dinner." Jo turned the small tool over in her hand.

"It will only make matters worse for me and the others will think I'm a nark."

Despite Jo wanting to nip any potential issues in the bud, Raylene had a valid point. Bringing it up could create even more hostility toward the woman. "Are you sure it's settled?"

"It's settled. As for the tool, that is not mine."

Jo was silent as she met the woman's gaze. Maybe she was being a fool, but she believed Raylene. She slipped the tool into her back pocket and stood. "I want to believe you, but I found this in your room. I'll let you off with a warning, but if I ever find another contraband item in your possession, you'll be asked to leave immediately."

Raylene swallowed hard and nodded. "I understand. Thank you for the second chance. Well, I guess I'm working on my third chance now."

Jo's expression softened. "I believe some of us do need a third chance. I know I have. I'll finish looking around."

Despite Jo's belief that Raylene was telling the truth, she checked every nook and cranny of the small bedroom and even removed the mattress to check underneath it.

Satisfied there was nothing else to find, Jo finished her inspections of the other units and then returned to the house.

Delta was in the kitchen, pounding a ball of bread dough. "And if I ever see that nasty woman again." She punched the dough. "I will give her something to complain about."

Jo snuck up behind her. "Still cranked up about Ms. Holcomb?" Her grin widened when Delta turned around, her face smudged with flour and her eyes burning.

"Looking back, I should've given that woman a piece of my mind."

"She's bitter and angry." Jo waved dismissively. "We've got bigger fish to fry than to worry about her."

"You're right. It just makes me angry. I suppose you heard about the disagreement between Raylene and a couple of the other women earlier today."

"Yes." Jo sank into a kitchen chair. "I planned to bring it up at dinner, but Raylene begged me not to, claiming it would only make matters worse."

"She's right. They'll only resent her even more. I think she's gonna have a tough time here until she finds somewhere else to go."

Jo nodded absentmindedly. Raylene had not been welcomed with open arms, and she felt somewhat responsible. The woman had gotten off on the wrong foot, and Jo was at a loss as to how to fix it.

She thought about mentioning the multi-purpose tool she found under Raylene's dresser, but remembered how her friend had also opposed Raylene from the get-go. Instead, she decided to keep the matter between the two of them.

"I've got some free time." Jo slid out of the chair and grabbed an apron off the hook. "I need something to take my mind off all that's going on around here. Put me to work."

Delta handed her friend her beloved and well-worn recipe book. "I've decided to make a batch of my chocolate chip banana nut muffins."

Jo could almost taste the melt-in-your-mouth chocolate and creamy banana muffin and her mouth started to water. "What's the occasion?"

The muffins were a treat, something Delta had made just once since moving in with Jo. She insisted they were only for special occasions, using the phrase, "Too much of a good thing and the specialness wears off."

"No occasion. I've been craving them, so I decided to make a batch for the bakery and a few extra to munch on around the house."

"Let me guess...Gary mentioned he loves muffins," Jo said.

"Maybe. I figured anything I can do to help the poor man feel better and get back on his feet is a good thing for us."

"Hmm." Jo didn't add to her comment but was beginning to suspect Delta had developed a soft spot for their gardener.

She mixed the muffin ingredients in a large bowl while Delta greased the muffin pans. During renovations, Jo had a commercial grade kitchen installed, knowing she would need some heavy-duty kitchen equipment to run a baked goods store.

It was paying off in spades, and Delta used every square inch of space. While the women worked, they discussed the recent string of incidents.

Jo poured the batter in the tins and watched Delta slide them into the oven. "I don't know what to think."

"I hate to even say this, but what if one of our own is behind the incidents?" Delta asked. "I watch some of those in-depth investigative shows on television." She tapped the side of her forehead. "We gotta try to put ourselves in the shoes of the culprit. They're always mentioning motive and opportunity."

"I..." Jo's voice trailed off. It was possible one of the women was behind the incidents. The opportunity was there. Plenty of opportunity to smash her mailbox, opportunity to try to break into the mercantile and possibly even to sneak up on Gary and attack him, right under Jo's nose, but why?

Delta threw out another theory. "Or maybe there are two culprits."

Jo untied the apron and hung it on the hook. "Perhaps Deputy Franklin will be able to help us get to the bottom of what's going on."

There was a creak overhead, and she glanced up. "Sounds like your patient is getting restless."

"I'll be lucky if I can keep him in bed until tomorrow morning." Delta ran upstairs to check on Gary while Jo roamed aimlessly around the house.

Not only did she have to worry about the vandalism incident, the attempted break-in at the mercantile and Gary's attack, but now she had to worry about the women getting along, too.

Raylene and Delta both thought it was a bad idea to bring up the disagreement at dinner, but perhaps if she could talk to them one on one, she could clear the air and potentially head off another incident.

Deciding this was the best course of action, Jo headed to Nash's workshop. She rapped lightly on the door and stepped inside.

Nash gave Jo a frantic look and tossed a tarp on top of his work area. "Jo...what are you doing here?"

The room reeked of varnish. Jo waved a hand across her face. "Good grief, Nash. You should open the door and vent this place before you pass out."

"It is kinda strong. I'll open the windows after you leave."

"You don't have a helper this afternoon?"

"Michelle left to go get me some stuff in the barn. She'll be back soon."

"Shoot. I wanted to chat with her. I'll come back later."

"You can't do that," Nash said.

"Why not?"

"Because I'm working on a special project. It's top secret."

"A special project?" Jo stepped closer, eyeing the tarp with interest. "What kind of top secret special project?"

"If I told you, it wouldn't be top secret anymore," Nash teased. "Now shoo. I'll send Michelle to track you down in a little while."

Despite Jo's attempt to get Nash to spill the beans, he was adamant she had to leave. Finally, she gave up. "Well, I guess I'll find out eventually. Please promise me you'll get some air circulating in here."

Nash's eyes twinkled mischievously as he lifted his hand in a mock salute. "Will do."

Jo could feel his eyes following her as she made her way out. She quietly closed the door behind her, thinking how she'd never noticed how blue his eyes were before.

She gave herself a mental shake, forcing Nash and his blue eyes from her mind as she made her rounds, chatting with as many of the women as she possibly could.

As the chats wore on, she was relieved to discover that, for the most part, the women got along just fine. Of course, there were minor issues such as having to wait for the showers or someone claiming another wouldn't do their fair share and take out the trash or clean up after themselves.

When Jo pointedly asked about Raylene, the answers were vague. She suspected that at least a couple of the women harbored some resentment for the newest member of the household.

Dinner was a quiet affair. Nash joined them, as was his typical routine whenever possible. Jo teased him about the secret project Michelle and he were working on, but the man refused to take the bait and changed the subject.

After dinner, several of the women hung out in the living room. Julie, Kelli and Michelle left, claiming they wanted to use the computers and watch television.

The conversation turned to the recent string of disturbing events.

"How is Gary?" Sherry asked.

"Delta is nursing him back to health and fattening him up," Jo teased. "I think he might make it downstairs sometime tomorrow if Delta hasn't tied him to the bed."

"I would never do that," Delta huffed. "He needs rest."

"I agree, and he couldn't be in better hands." Jo changed the subject. "What do you think about us taking a self-defense class?"

"I like the idea," Sherry said.

"Me too," Leah, another of the residents, chimed in.

"I'll start looking for someone tomorrow."

It wasn't long before the women excused themselves, leaving Delta and Jo alone.

Delta struggled to her feet. "I'm going to check on Gary one last time, and then hit the hay. Seven o'clock will be here before you know it."

Jo wished her friend a good night and then turned the television on. She flipped through the channels. Nothing caught her eye, so she shut it back off.

Duke, whose favorite spot was sleeping on top of Jo's feet, rolled over.

"I guess it's just you and me, Duke. Why don't we head outside for a breath of fresh air before we turn in?" Jo set the remote on the coffee table and made her way out onto the porch.

The cool evening air was a welcome relief from the day's stifling heat. Off in the distance, the crickets continued their nighttime serenade.

Duke waited until Jo settled on the swing. He stuck both paws on the bench planning to join her when he abruptly stopped. He dropped back down, his head whipped around and he let out a low growl, staring out into the dark night.

The hair on the back of Jo's neck stood up, and she got the distinct feeling they were being watched.

# Chapter 14

Jo sprang from the swing and flipped off the porchlight. "Who's there?"

Duke trotted to the top of the steps, his ears straight up and on high alert. He let out another warning growl.

*Snap.* Jo's breath caught in her throat when she heard the snap, followed by a rustling. She squinted her eyes, peering into the dark night.

"Jo...are you out here?"

Jo stumbled back, almost colliding with Duke. "Delta?"

"Yeah. I was on my way to my room when I saw the porch light go off." The screen door creaked loudly as Delta joined her. "What are you doing out here in the dark?"

"Duke and I heard something. There's someone out there."

"Let's get back inside." Delta grabbed Duke's collar and coaxed him inside.

Jo hurriedly followed behind. She slammed the front door and flipped the deadbolt. "Tomorrow morning, Nash is going to run to the hardware store and pick up some motion sensor lights and surveillance cameras."

"I think it's time." Delta nodded toward the porch. "Were you able to see anything?"

"No. I just sat down when Duke let out a growl, and the hair on the back of my neck stood straight up. Someone is out there," Jo insisted. "They were watching me, so I flipped the porch light off."

"You shoulda hollered for help. Someone could've attacked you."

"I wasn't thinking," Jo said. "Along with surveillance cameras, I'm wondering if maybe it's time to polish up the old handgun and take it out for a few practice shots."

"You read my mind. I was thinking the same thing. Let's run out back tomorrow after breakfast and do a little target practice." Delta patted Duke's head. "In the meantime, we'll leave Duke down here to keep an eye on the place. He'll let us know if he hears something."

Duke preferred to sleep at the foot of Jo's bed, but Delta was right. Duke not only had a sharp sniffer, but he also had a sharp ear and was generally a good guard dog.

Jo dragged her pup's doggie bed into the living room and placed it in front of the door.

Duke gave her a pitiful look and a grunt of protest.

"I'm sorry, Duke. You have to sleep here tonight, to guard us."

She gave him a handful of doggie treats. "Keep an eye open and an ear tuned." Jo gave him a quick pat and then headed to her room, passing by Gary's room on her way to her own. The door was ajar, and she could see the soft glow of the nightlight.

Careful not to disturb him, she tiptoed past to the end of the hall and her master suite. During renovations, Jo had a couple of the walls knocked out and claimed one of the upstairs bathrooms for herself.

She'd retained as much of the original charm as she could and was pleased with the results. After brushing her teeth and washing her face, she donned a pair of shorts and a t-shirt, in the event she needed to confront an intruder.

She folded the sheets back and cast a quick glance at her drawn shades, wondering if whoever had been watching her was still out there.

"Better safe than sorry." Jo unlocked her bedside table, grabbed her loaded gun and gingerly set it on the nightstand.

After saying her prayers, she tucked the covers under her chin and stared sightlessly into the darkness. Who was lurking outside her home? It may have been a small animal or maybe even a deer passing through...or perhaps it was something more sinister.

A shiver ran down Jo's spine. No, she was certain someone had been out there, watching her, watching Duke. They hadn't done anything, although there had been ample time for someone to spring from the shadows and attack her.

Duke would've slowed them down, but if the person had a weapon, eventually Jo and her beloved dog would've been injured, or worse.

What if Delta was right? What if there was more than one person targeting her and the farm? What if it was one of the women?

She quickly dismissed the thought. Surely, it wasn't one of her own. Jo thought of Raylene's divine intervention. Jumping off the bridge was a surefire suicide mission. So how did she live? Had God sent angels to step in and save her?

She remembered Raylene's comment that she told God she was sorry right before she jumped. Lastly, Jo thought of her own divine intervention, which could very well have saved her life the night of the fire.

Unable to sleep, Jo climbed back out of bed and crept down the stairs to her computer. She once read that certain areas were hot spots for supernatural occurrences.

Was Divine, Kansas, the center of the forty-eight lower states, a haven for otherworldly beings? Had God chosen Divine as a location for angelic visitations? Other people in the area seemed to believe so.

Jo turned her computer on and began searching the internet. Although she couldn't find specifics on Divine, she found several stories of others reporting angelic encounters in the area. Jo opened her online Bible and searched for verses on angels.

She scrolled the screen and clicked on Hebrews 13:2:

**"Be not forgetful to entertain strangers: for thereby some have entertained angels unawares."** Hebrews 13:2 King James Version (KJV)

She studied several more verses and finally shut the computer off. If God had sent angels to Divine, to Raylene and to her, then surely, he would protect them from whatever evil lurked outside her doors.

Duke, who had joined her during her search, followed her out of the office. She stopped him at the bottom of the stairs. This time, he didn't pin her with his sorrowful gaze. Instead, he crawled into his bed.

"Good boy, Duke. Tomorrow, you get a special treat," Jo promised.

She returned to her room and quickly drifted off to sleep. Jo woke early the next morning feeling rested and at peace. God was in control of her circumstances, both the good and bad.

Delta was already in the kitchen when Jo got there. "Thanks for the coffee." She poured a cup and eyed her friend, standing in front of the stove. "Do you still want to practice shooting this morning?"

"Yes, if you want to."

"I think we should."

Delta cast Jo a sideways glance. "I heard you downstairs after I went to bed. I figured you were still concerned over last night's scare."

"I couldn't shake the thought of someone outside watching me, so I decided to do a little research on my computer." Jo sipped the hot coffee. "Do you believe in angels?"

"Of course I do. I also believe in guardian angels." Delta smiled. "You got yours working overtime."

"Without a doubt." Jo wandered to the kitchen window and looked out. "I think I'll give Pastor

Murphy a call this morning, to see if he's had any luck finding a place for Raylene."

"I can't say as I blame you. We have enough troubles without having the women at each other's throats." Delta poured pancake batter on the hot griddle, and it sizzled. "You got a big heart, Jo Pepperdine."

"Sometimes I wonder if I'm doing God's calling or if I opened this place to ease my own guilt."

Delta set the bowl of batter on the counter and eyed her friend thoughtfully. "It could be a little of both. Either way, if God is in it, and I do believe he is, then all of this will work out. Whether the deputies will get to the bottom of what's going on around here, and justice will eventually be served remains to be seen."

Jo helped Delta finish making breakfast. During the meal, she paid special attention to how the women interacted, not only with Raylene but also with one another.

The women seemed, if not friendly, at least polite. Of course, it was possible if there were hard feelings or grudges they were keeping it to themselves while Jo and Delta were around.

They discussed the day's schedules, and after finishing their food, the women made quick work of cleaning up.

While they cleaned, Jo headed to her office to give the pastor a call. She left a brief message and sorted through some unpaid bills before wandering back into the kitchen.

Jo made it as far as the doorway and abruptly stopped, unsure of where to look first...at the array of arsenal covering the kitchen table, or Delta's attire. She burst out laughing. "What on earth?"

Delta was seated at the table, surrounded by weaponry. She was clothed in camo, from the camo-colored bandana tied around her head to the short sleeve camo shirt and khaki colored shorts. A pair of steel-toed boots completed her ensemble.

"What's so funny?" Delta frowned.

"You. You look like…"

"I look like I'm going hunting. So sue me."

"I didn't mean to hurt your feelings," Jo apologized. "I don't think I've ever seen you in camo before. It's a good look."

Jo slowly walked to the table, perusing the array of weaponry. "Where did you get all of these?"

"Guns are kind of a hobby of mine." Delta picked up one of the handguns and began polishing it. "My dad taught me how to shoot a gun before I learned how to drive."

"No kidding."

"Here in America's Heartland, guns are a part of life, a part of the culture." Delta carefully placed the weapon in its case. "It's all about God, guns and country."

"I guess I never thought about it," Jo said.

"That's because you're a city slicker. You do know how to shoot a gun?"

"Yes, but it's never been a high priority on my list to practice." Jo pointed to a pearl-handled gun. "So what's the difference between this gun and some of the others?"

Delta started on a long spiel, explaining the difference in the weapons and their features. "This one is my favorite." She lifted a dull, gray/black handgun and held it up for Jo to inspect.

"This is a *Glock 26,* nicknamed the 'Baby Glock.' It's a subcompact 9mm, kinda clunky and not as pretty as some of the others, but this baby can't be beat for reliability. It'll fire even if it's coated in mud or soaking wet."

Jo lifted a brow as she eyed the guns. She wouldn't describe any gun as "pretty," but then collecting weaponry wasn't Jo's hobby.

Delta handed her the gun. "It's not as comfortable as some of the others, but like I said, this one will do the job."

Jo quickly inspected the gun and handed it back. "I'll take your word for it."

"Do you want to shoot one of my guns or bring your own?"

"I think I should bring mine. I'll be right back."

"Don't forget to grab a round of bullets, too. If you run out, you can use my gun. I'll bring some extra. I have plenty," Delta called out.

"I bet you do," Jo muttered under her breath. She ran upstairs to get her gun and returned moments later.

"Whatcha got?" Delta eyed Jo's gun with interest.

"I have no idea. The salesmen who sold it to me said it was a good gun for a woman." Jo handed her gun to her friend.

"Not bad." Delta balanced the weapon in her hand. "This is a *Ruger LC9s*. It's a good carry gun. See how compact and lightweight it is? You can hide this gem in your purse or pocket, and no one will ever know."

"I don't plan on carrying it around," Jo said. "I bought it a while ago, thinking if I lived out here in the middle of nowhere, I might need to protect myself."

"And judging by what's going on around here lately, you made the right decision." Delta handed the gun back before carefully placing her gun inside the case and snapping the lid shut. "You don't have a gun case?"

"No. I keep the gun secured in my nightstand."

"I think I'll bring my *Glock 26*. Let me put the other guns away in my locked cabinet." Delta shut the gun cases, stacked them on top of each other and carried them to her room.

On her way back, she grabbed a plastic garbage bag. "I have the targets ready to go."

"Where are we going?" Jo asked.

"I figured the best spot was out near the larger back garden, along the fence line. We can use the old pile of firewood as a backstop to catch the bullets."

"That's a good idea." Jo fell into step with Delta. "I left a message for Pastor Murphy to call me."

"I think you're making the right decision," Delta said.

"I hope so." Jo still wasn't convinced, especially after last night. If God sent angels to intervene on Raylene's behalf, perhaps she was meant to be in Divine.

The women reached the back corner of the property and the barbed wire fence dividing Jo's property from David Kilwin's farm. On the other side of the fence were rows of leafy green vegetables for as far as the eye could see.

The deer loved the farm fields and Jo's gardens so much that the garden-loving creatures had become a nuisance.

Delta set her gun case and the bag of cans next to the row of sunflowers before making her way to the woodpile. She balanced one of the cans on top of a piece of wood.

Jo trudged behind, eyeing the can with interest. "What is this?"

"It's our target practice."

"There's a face." Jo chuckled. "And hair. You created your own tin can targets."

"It's the only way I can focus. These are the bad guys. It helps when I make a face; you know...bullseye and all of that."

"You're full of surprises," Jo teased. "Since you're the expert, you go first."

"You'll want these." Delta fished inside her pocket, pulled out a pair of earplugs and handed them to Jo.

"Thank you. You thought of everything." Jo wiggled an earplug in each ear and moved away, giving Delta a wide berth.

Delta removed her gun from the case. She slid the safety and inspected the chamber before centering her stance and lifting the gun. She took careful aim, closing one eye as she focused on the tin can.

*Pop. Pop.*

Delta fired off a couple of shots. The first bullet grazed the can and the second was dead center. The can rocketed skyward before landing a short distance away.

"Wow! That was impressive."

"I should've nailed it first try. It's been a while. I guess I'm a little rusty," Delta said. "Your turn." She shifted to the right and stood behind Jo.

"Here goes nothing." Jo sucked in a breath and lifted the gun. She squeezed one eye shut, keeping a tight grip on the gun as she eased the trigger back. The force of the discharge sent her stumbling backward. "Umpf."

"Rookie mistake." Delta closed her eyes and shook her head. "You need to balance your weight and brace yourself."

"Okay." Jo aligned her feet with her hips and locked her knees before lifting the gun again. She pulled the trigger.

*Pop*.

It was another clear miss.

"Your aim is too high!" Delta hollered. "You gotta come down a little."

Jo nodded and lowered the weapon. She fired off another shot. This time, the bullet hit the top of the can, sending it sailing in the air where it landed on the other side of the fence. She lowered the gun. "Finally…I finally hit it."

The women took turns shooting at the cans until the bag was empty.

After they finished, Jo collected the cans while Delta placed them back in the bag. "We should practice at least once a week."

"I agree. Once I got the hang of it, it was kinda fun."

"I have an archery set, too, if you're interested."

Jo wrinkled her nose. "Uh...I'll think about it." She thanked Delta for the shooting lesson and then headed upstairs to lock her gun in her dresser drawer.

Her cell phone was sitting on top. She glanced at the screen and noticed she'd missed a call. It was Pastor Murphy. There was no message, so she dialed his number.

"Pastor Murphy speaking."

"Hi, Pastor Murphy. This is Jo Pepperdine. I'm sorry I missed your call."

"No worries. I got your message and planned to give you a call. I have an update on Raylene."

# Chapter 15

"You haven't been able to find a place for her yet," Jo guessed.

"I'm still working on it, but I have a solid lead. There's a spot opening up in a large group home in Kansas City."

Jo's heart sank. After extensive research into the lives of former female convicts, she knew that living in the city and moving into a large group home was double trouble. The odds of Raylene successfully starting over after entering a larger facility in the city was nearly cut in half.

"There's nowhere else? No smaller halfway house or women's place outside the city that might be able to take her?"

"I haven't found one yet. In fact, we're lucky this place is even considering her. Like you, they don't take certain convicted felons," the pastor said. "I'm still trying."

"It's only been a couple of days," Jo pointed out. "Thank you for staying on top of it."

"How is it going with Raylene?"

Jo detected a hint of hope in the pastor's voice. "It's okay. As far as I know, there has only been one minor incident between her and one of the other women." Jo didn't mention finding the multi-purpose tool. If there was any inkling of breaking the rules, she knew the pastor would suspend his search for finding a place for her to go, and Raylene would be on her own.

"It's a period of adjustment. I'm sure there has been some pushback over allowing her to stay."

"Yes." Jo didn't elaborate, and the pastor didn't ask. She thanked him again for continuing to work on Raylene's behalf and then told him good-bye.

Jo spent the next couple of hours inventorying the mercantile merchandise. The inventory was getting low, and she would need to find more soon.

According to Marlee, summer and fall were the busy seasons. During the winter months, the number of visitors to the area dwindled, so she knew she needed to amass a cushion of cash for the leaner months.

Delta kept the bakery well stocked, and Sherry assured Jo she checked daily to make sure they weren't selling expired goods. To entice patrons to purchase, Jo had recently added a tasting tray. Since the addition, baked goods sales had skyrocketed.

"I see Delta put out her chocolate chip and banana muffins." Jo pointed to the sample slices of muffins on the tasting tray.

"They're delicious." Sherry patted her tummy. "I taste-tested one."

Jo grabbed the tongs and selected a small sliver. She popped the tender morsel into her mouth, savoring a chunk of chocolate mingled with creamy banana. "They're perfect."

"And flying off the shelves." Sherry pointed to the half-empty display tray. "We'll be sold out within a couple of hours."

A woman carried a basketful of goodies to the counter and set them on top. Jo greeted the woman before exiting the store. Her last stop was Nash's workshop.

She nearly collided with him as he was on his way out, the farm's truck keys in hand. "Hey, Jo."

"Hey, Nash. Are you leaving?"

"I'm heading into town to shop for surveillance cameras and motion lights. Delta cornered me first thing this morning. She said something about you being out on the porch last night, and you heard some noises."

"Yes. I almost forgot. Duke heard it, too. It scared the dickens out of me."

"It's high time we installed some security equipment," Nash said. "I talked to Wayne over at *Tool Time Hardware* in Divine. He said he has a decent inventory of security stuff."

"Do you mind if I tag along?"

"Of course not. I would love the company, plus you need to get out more."

"You sound like Delta." Jo held up a finger. "Let me grab my purse. I'll be right back."

She dashed inside and up the stairs. On her way back out, she hollered into the kitchen to let Delta know she was riding into town with Nash.

Delta poked her head around the corner. "Good for you. About time you got outta my hair for a while."

Nash had already pulled the truck around and was waiting for Jo near the front steps. She slipped into the passenger seat. "I've never been inside the hardware store."

"You'll like it. Wayne has a lot more than just tools and gadgets."

During the drive to town, Nash and Jo discussed the recent string of incidents. They talked about life at the farm and then she asked him how his apartment was working out.

"I love it. It's perfect for me. I love working with you and the women. I feel like I'm actually doing something that will make a difference."

"Helping the women get back on their feet," Jo said.

"Yes. I feel like I won the lottery. Not only have you given me room and board, plus a salary and a percentage of the sales on my woodworking stuff, Delta's home cooked meals are the best." Nash smacked his lips. "The woman sure does know how to cook."

"Yes, she does."

Nash grew quiet for a moment. "I feel like I found my purpose in life. I get a chance to talk to the women when they're helping me in the workshop. Almost all of them have troubled pasts."

"Yes, they do." Jo had heard all of their stories, and could almost feel the women's pain as they talked about their pasts.

"They have been through a lot." Jo studied her hands in her lap. "Maybe that's why I'm so passionate about trying to give them a second chance."

"And they love you for it," Nash said quietly. "Raylene told me she won't be staying."

"No." Jo sucked in a breath. "I broke my own rules by letting her stay. I think it's caused a little conflict."

"Not that my two cents matters, but I think you did the right thing by letting her stay." Nash pulled to the stop sign and looked both ways before continuing. "Do you think there's a chance you'll change your mind?"

"I wish I could, but I don't see how that's possible."

"It's a shame. She seems like a perfect fit." Nash turned onto Main Street and eased the truck into an empty parking spot. "We're here."

Jo joined him on the sidewalk, and he held the door as she stepped inside.

The brick store reminded Jo of an old factory. The inside smelled of fresh paint mingled with citrus.

Near the front were bins of door pulls, nuts, bolts, screws and every other imaginable hardware item.

Beyond the bins and to the left was an array of power tools. On the right were gardening supplies and closer to the back were wooden barrels, overflowing with hard candy.

Jo slowed as she passed by the barrels. "I used to love these hard candies." She grabbed a paper bag from the stack and began placing pieces inside.

"I'll be over there." Nash pointed to some racks on the other side of the store.

"I'll be along shortly." Jo dumped a large scoop of cinnamon candy disks in the bottom of the bag. Another scoop of peppermint star brites, strawberry bon bons, root beer barrels and butterscotch disks followed.

By the time Jo finished, there was barely enough room to fold the top. She set the scoop in the holder and joined Nash, who stood off to one side talking to a short, stocky man.

"Wayne, this is my boss, Joanna Pepperdine. Jo, this is Wayne Malton, the owner of *Tool Time Hardware*."

Wayne smiled widely as he shook Jo's hand. "So you're the infamous Jo Pepperdine. I've heard a lot about you."

"Bad, I'm sure," Jo muttered.

"Nah. The only person I've heard complaining is that old sourpuss, Deb Holcomb, and she doesn't count." Wayne released his grip. "There are plenty of us town folks who think you're doing a wonderful thing out there at the farm. You have our support."

"Thank you." A warm flush crept into Jo's cheeks. "I need all the support I can get."

Jo's throat clogged at the unexpected compliment, and she quickly changed the subject. "I'm sure Nash told you we're looking for motion lights and maybe a surveillance camera or two."

"Yes, and I was telling him you're in luck. We started carrying the *Top Notch Security* brand. I use these here at the store and highly recommend them." Wayne began discussing the technical aspects of *Top Notch*, which went over Jo's head.

After he finished, Nash turned to Jo. "Well? What do you think? If I install a motion light in both the front and back of the house, along with one in front of the mercantile and the bakeshop, plus two surveillance cameras, it's going to cost a pretty penny."

"And worth every single one," Jo said. "If you think it will work for us, you have my blessing. It also wouldn't hurt to have a smaller surveillance camera, which could be moved around for temporary surveillance."

"That's a great idea," Nash said.

"I have one that's a cheaper model and user friendly," Wayne said. "As for the other equipment, it's fairly easy to install."

The men carried the boxes to the checkout and Jo trailed behind. After paying for the purchases, Jo thanked Wayne for his input, and the couple wandered out of the store.

"I'm sorry it cost so much, Jo," Nash apologized.

"Like I said, if this equipment works, it will be worth every penny."

Back at the property, Jo helped Nash carry the purchases into the workshop. "Let me know if you need help installing the equipment."

"Will do. I want to take a closer look at the instructions to make sure I have all of the tools needed."

Jo thanked Nash for letting her tag along and then stepped out of the workshop. Her plan was to check on Gary before beginning her shift at the bakeshop.

"Jo!" Julie raced around the corner of the building, waving her arms frantically.

"Hey, Julie."

"I'm sorry to bother you, but we've got a big problem over at the mercantile."

# Chapter 16

"What is going on?"

"Raylene and I were getting ready to switch shifts when a customer needed help over by the dressing rooms. She offered to watch my cash register. When I came back, I counted the money, and the numbers don't add up. There's money missing."

"Let me see if I can help." Jo hurried after Julie. "Do you think Raylene took money from the cash register while you weren't looking?"

"I *know* she took money." Julie held the door, and Jo stepped inside.

She made a beeline for the back where a red-faced Raylene stood waiting. "I didn't do it."

"Julie claims you were keeping an eye on the cash register while she helped a customer. When she

238

finished, she counted the money so you could take the next shift and there's money missing."

"So she says." Raylene's eyes sparked with anger. "I was here for less than five minutes."

"Five minutes is plenty of time to steal," Julie said.

"Search me." Raylene's hands shot up in the air. "Go ahead."

Several shoppers paused to watch the exchange, and Jo lowered her voice. "Let's discuss this outdoors." She turned to Julie. "Can you watch the store for a little longer?"

"Of course."

Raylene marched to the exit. She waited for Jo to join her on the front porch. "She's lying."

"I don't know what to think."

"Do you think I would be dumb enough to steal money?"

"Why would Julie lie?"

"Because she's an angry, bitter woman."

Jo started pacing, her mind whirling. Was Raylene intentionally stirring up trouble? She had another, equally concerning thought.

"There's something else." Raylene cleared her throat. "I had a problem with a customer while I was watching the register. She claims I short-changed her. I know I didn't. Finally, she left."

Jo stopped pacing. "Tell me everything that happened, from the moment you arrived to take over for Julie."

"I just got there and was waiting for Julie to count out the money and swap places. Right around that time, a woman was having trouble with the dressing room door, so Julie offered to help her. She asked me to watch the register. I waited for her to come back. She counted the money, and that's when she said there was money missing and she went to find you."

Jo rubbed a weary hand across her brow. It was one woman's word against the other...and the other - Raylene - already had strikes against her. It was too much for Jo.

"You believe Julie," Raylene said in a quiet voice. "I never meant to cause trouble." Before Jo could reply, the woman turned on her heel. She trudged to the end of the walkway and disappeared around the side of the building.

Jo started to go after her but stopped. She needed to sort through the latest mess, but first she needed to ask Julie to cover the store for a little longer.

She went back inside and waited for Julie to finish ringing up a customer. "No problem. I'll stay for as long as you need me."

"Thank you." Jo stopped by the bakeshop on her way out. Michelle, the resident working behind the counter, gave Jo a troubled look and motioned her over.

"I-I'm sorry to bother you, Jo. There's a problem with one of the customers. She wants to return some baked goods she claims are rancid. She also said she purchased some merchandise in the mercantile and the woman working short-changed her."

Jo's heart sank. "Did she remember the clerk's name?" Although Jo asked the question, she already knew the answer.

Michelle shifted uncomfortably. "It was Raylene. She described her to a 'T.'"

"Where is the customer who claims she was short-changed and is complaining about the baked goods?"

"Over there." Michelle pointed to a woman standing with her back to her and clutching a bakery bag.

Jo's heart plummeted when she recognized the woman. It was Debbie Holcomb. Her first instinct was to bolt. Instead, she squared her shoulders and made her way across the room. "I hear you have a complaint about our baked goods."

The woman slowly turned, an evil grin on her face. Holcomb thrust the bag of baked goods toward Jo. "I purchased some baked goods at your store a short time ago. When I got home, I discovered they were rancid."

"All of our baked goods are made fresh daily."

"Not these."

Jo opened the top of the bag. "Which ones are bad?"

"All of them," Holcomb smirked. "And I'll have you know your nitwit employee over in the store short-changed me. She had trouble counting out the money and got me flustered. I thought we straightened it out. When I arrived home, I realized she shorted me five dollars."

"You can't be serious," Jo said bluntly.

"Are you accusing me of lying?" The woman's shrill voice rose an octave.

"I am doing no such thing," Jo replied in an even voice.

"This is a shady operation you're running here." Holcomb ranted on about selling expired goods and stealing from customers.

Jo stomped over to the cash register. She punched in the access code, grabbed a twenty-dollar bill and thrust it toward her. "Get out and don't ever come back."

Holcomb's jaw dropped. "Y-you can't talk to me like that."

"Get out before I throw you out."

The woman snatched the money out of Jo's hand and backed out of the store. "You won't get away with treating me like this." Holcomb slammed the door behind her, the threat hanging in the air.

"What an obnoxious woman," Michelle said.

"Among other things. If she ever steps foot in the store again, call the police." Jo followed Holcomb out. She watched the woman peel out of the parking lot and careen onto the road. "Good riddance."

Jo plodded back to the house where Delta stood waiting on the front porch. "What was that all about?"

"Debbie Holcomb and more." Jo's shoulders sagged. "It's a mess. I'm going to grab a cup of coffee, and then I'll tell you what happened."

Over coffee, Jo poured out the sordid story, starting with Julie's accusation that Raylene took money from the cash register and ending with her kicking Debbie Holcomb out of the store.

"Man," Delta chuckled. "I would've loved to have seen the look on Holcomb's face."

"I told her never to come back." Jo cradled her coffee cup. "What should I do about Raylene?"

"You know my thoughts," Delta said. "I was against letting her stay in the first place. We've had nothing but trouble."

"We were having trouble before she came along," Jo sighed. "It's just multiplying."

"Three strikes and you're out."

"There's something not sitting right about the whole thing." Jo slipped out of her chair and wandered to the window. "Raylene wasn't here for the vandalism incidents or Gary's attack."

"True, but she was involved in a dust-up with one of the other women and now the missing money from the cash register," Delta pointed out. "She's definitely got two strikes against her."

Technically, there were three if Jo counted the contraband multi-purpose tool she found under Raylene's nightstand. "We really have no choice. She's going to have to leave. I'll go talk to her."

"Would you like me to go with you?" Delta asked.

"It might not be a bad idea. Let me think about what I want to say first." Jo finished her coffee and wandered into her office. She attempted to take care of some paperwork, but she couldn't focus because her thoughts were on Raylene.

Finally, she gave up and returned to the kitchen.

"I forgot to tell you. Gary and I were talking about his attack, and he might have some new information," Delta said. "He's awake if you want to go talk to him."

"Absolutely. You mean there might be some good news today?" Jo hurried up the stairs. She rapped lightly on Gary's bedroom door.

"Come in."

Jo stepped inside and found him sitting upright in bed, the television remote in his hand. "Delta told me you thought you might have remembered something about your attack."

"Yep. I've been thinking about it a lot. Remember when I told you, I thought I smelled something funny inside the shed?"

"Yeah. You went in to investigate, heard a noise and next thing you knew, you woke up in the ambulance."

"Right." Gary nodded. "And I remember what I smelled. Pot."

"Pot?" Jo shifted her feet.

"You know...marijuana, like a lingering smell, not overpowering."

Jo tiptoed to the edge of his bed. "Are you sure?"

"Yep. Have you checked the shed since my attack?"

"No. I..." Jo's mind whirled. "Other than sticking my head in the door, I didn't venture in to have a look around. It's been one crisis right after another the last couple of days. I'm going to as soon as I leave here."

Gary plucked at the covers. "You think one of the residents might be hiding marijuana or smoking it in the shed?"

"Anything is possible." Drugs were a definite no-no, even over-the-counter medications, which required either Delta or Jo's permission to dispense. "Is there anything else?"

"No. That's it," Gary said. "Other than thank you for letting me recuperate here. This place is like staying in a five star resort. Delta is spoiling me rotten, and I feel a little guilty."

Jo patted his hand. "Don't feel guilty. She loves every minute of it, and we love having you here." She thanked Gary for the information and returned to the kitchen where Delta was taking pies out of the oven. "Well? Did Gary remember something useful?"

"Yep. He said he smelled pot...marijuana."

"Marijuana?" Delta nearly dropped the pie on the counter. "Someone is smoking pot in the shed?"

"Maybe." Jo ran a ragged hand through her hair. "He mentioned smelling something odd in the shed the day I visited him in the hospital. With everything going on, I completely forgot about it."

"We need to search the shed." Delta finished removing the pies and tossed her oven mitts on the counter.

When they reached the shed, Jo cautiously opened the door. Light poured in from the doorway, illuminating the interior.

Delta crowded in behind her. "Do you smell anything?"

"I don't know." Jo took a tentative step inside, sniffing the air. It smelled damp. She took another step and the faint, yet distinct odor of marijuana hung in the air. "I smell it."

"Gross." Delta sniffed loudly. "It smells like skunk."

"Right," Jo said.

"So it's not pot."

"It is pot...pot sometimes smells like skunk," Jo explained.

Delta snorted. "I never touched the stuff. Call me crazy, but why would someone enjoy smoking something that smells like skunk?"

"You pose an excellent question." Jo flipped the switch on the wall, casting a dull yellow light. The shelves were crammed full of gardening tools, seeds, mulch, along with an array of other gadgets. "We better start searching."

"I'll start on this side, you start on the other." Delta reached for a watering can.

"Divide and conquer." Jo and Delta worked quickly, removing the items on the shelves, starting from the top and working their way to the bottom. They finished the side shelves and then moved to the back shelf.

The women started at the top again, working their way down. They reached the bottom shelf and again, found nothing.

Jo brushed the dirt off her hands. "I don't get it. I can smell it."

"Maybe it was a skunk," Delta said.

"Right." Jo walked to the door and reached for the light switch, her eyes falling on the middle shelf. "Wait a minute..."

She dropped to her knees and peered under the bottom shelf.

"What are you doing?" Delta asked.

"We didn't search *under* the cabinets." Jo cautiously reached under the cabinet and cringed when she touched a bug carcass. She ran her hand along the bottom. "Nothing."

Jo stuck her hand under the second shelf, leaning in to reach all the way to the back where she felt something smooth. "I...think I found something. It's a bag." She sucked in a breath before shoving her hand all the way to the back. She grabbed the plastic and gave it a sharp tug.

"I have it." Jo wiggled backward and shifted to a sitting position to inspect the clear plastic bag and its contents. "Bingo!"

"Pot?" Delta leaned over her shoulder.

"Without a doubt." Jo opened the pouch and cautiously sniffed the contents. "Yes. This is definitely marijuana."

"Now what?"

Jo stared at the bag someone, quite possibly one of the residents had hidden inside the garden shed. But who?

Delta echoed her own thoughts. "How are we gonna figure out who hid this?"

"I..." Jo tapped the bag with her finger, an idea beginning to form in her head. "I have an idea."

Jo returned the marijuana to its original hiding place and followed Delta out of the shed. She turned the light off and closed the door. "At dinner tonight, I'm going to announce that we're cleaning out the shed while Gary recuperates."

"Ah." Delta rubbed her hands together. "Which will force the person who hid the drugs and possibly attacked Gary to sneak in there to get it."

"And we'll be waiting for them."

"A sting." Delta clapped her hands. "I love it."

"Me too, but first, I need to talk to Raylene."

Delta and Jo circled the buildings and stopped when they reached Raylene's apartment. The door was ajar. Jo eased it open and stuck her head inside.

"Hello? Raylene?"

The room was empty.

# Chapter 17

"I wonder if she took off." A wave of concern washed over Jo.

"I don't know. Before we send out a search party, let's have a look around. Maybe she went for a walk," Delta said.

"Right." Jo pulled the door closed behind her. They passed by the smaller garden and the bee boxes before heading to the other corner of the property and the larger garden.

They circled the silo. Delta was the first to spot her. "She's over there."

They found Raylene near the edge of the pond, her arms wrapped around her knees and staring at the water.

"Hey, Raylene." Delta plopped down on one side of her and Jo eased in on the other.

She gave them a quick glance. "Hey."

"After you left, a customer returned to the store, claiming you short-changed her," Jo said.

"She intentionally tried to fluster me. I counted her money back three times."

"The woman is...a troublemaker." Jo picked up a pebble and tossed it into the pond, watching the ripple spread out across the water.

"I know why you're here," Raylene said. "I've worn out my welcome, and the others resent me, at least some of them do."

"I think the problem is I bent the rules. They think I'm showing favoritism."

"I understand," Raylene said. "I was going to up and leave, but decided I should at least say 'good-bye' and thank you for taking me in."

Delta spoke. "Where are you gonna go?"

Raylene shrugged. "I don't know. I figured if God saved me, he would help me find a place to go." She turned to Jo, her expression somber. "Do you believe God saved me?"

"Yes, I do." Jo nodded. "He's given you a second chance, whether it's here, or somewhere else. God has a plan for your life, Raylene."

Raylene studied Jo's face before slowly nodding. "That's what I was thinking." She stared out at the water again. "If it's all right with you, I'm going to apologize to Julie before I leave."

"I think it would be a nice gesture," Jo said.

"When she stormed out and didn't come back right away, I figured the two of you were searching my room to see what else I might have taken. When she showed up with you, I knew I was toast."

Jo frowned. "Julie left you in charge of the store after arguing with you about the missing money, and she was gone for a while?"

"Yeah. Like I said, I figured you were searching my room. If you want to search it again, the door is unlocked."

"We didn't search your room. I thought Julie confronted you and then came to find me."

"Well, if she did, she took her sweet time doing it. She was gone a long time."

Jo thought back to the incident, how she was walking to the house and Julie called out to her as she ran toward her from behind the stores. "Now that you mention it, she was coming around the back of the building, not from the store."

"So maybe she snuck into my room to search it." Raylene dropped her chin on top of her knees.

"Wait a minute!" Jo scrambled to her feet. "Yesterday, during the incident with the medicine cabinets...was Julie the one who argued with you?"

"Yeah. She definitely resents me," Raylene said.

"Jo," Delta said. "Are you thinking what I'm thinking?"

"Thinking what?" Raylene asked.

"Nothing." Jo forced a smile. "I have a few things to check on. Please don't leave yet. Let's get through tonight, and then tomorrow we'll discuss your situation."

"Are you sure?" Raylene slowly stood. "I don't want to cause any more trouble."

"I don't see how that would even be possible."

Jo waited until Raylene left. "All of these incidents, the smashed mailbox, the break-in at the mercantile. Sherry remembered hearing noises outside her bedroom window the other morning around the time of the break-in and Gary's attack."

"Julie's unit is on the end, closest to the mercantile," Delta said. "All of the incidents happened not long after Julie got here."

"The other night when I felt like someone was out there watching me..." Jo thought about the bag of marijuana. "What if it was her?"

"We have no proof," Delta pointed out. "Although we do have a plan."

"I think there's a good chance Julie is the culprit." Jo lifted a finger. "All of the incidents occurred after she arrived."

"Yes," Delta nodded.

"Second, Sherry remembered hearing a clunking noise by her window the morning of the mercantile break-in. We recently installed the locks on the cabinets after there was an issue with some of the women and claims of missing toiletries."

"Because Julie said someone was taking her stuff." Delta slapped her knee. "It was Julie's idea for the locked medicine cabinets."

"You're right. It's high time I conduct a surprise inspection of the medicine cabinets," Jo stepped away from the pond. "I'm going to do it first thing tomorrow morning."

# Chapter 18

Delta returned to the house while Jo made a beeline for Nash's workshop. She would need his help in setting up the new surveillance camera inside the garden shed; something she hoped he could take care of before dinner, since that was when she planned to tell the women they would be cleaning the shed the following morning.

Thankfully, he was working alone. To say Nash was surprised by the discovery of the drugs was an understatement. "I had no idea. I never go into the garden shed. Are you sure it was marijuana?"

"Sure as sugar," Jo nodded. "We need the new portable surveillance camera installed inside the shed, but we have to do it without raising any suspicion. Do you think you can handle it?"

"Of course. I'll have it up and working within the hour," Nash promised. "You think you'll catch the culprit tonight?"

"Yes, especially after I tell them at dinner we're emptying the shed in the morning and cleaning it out to surprise Gary while he's recuperating."

"I want to help," Nash said.

"You are."

"No, I mean I want to help with the sting."

"Are you sure?"

"Sure as sugar," Nash teased. "Besides, I need to keep an eye on you and Delta, to keep you safe."

Jo's cheeks warmed. "Thanks, Nash. You're the best."

"You're welcome." He gave Jo's arm a light squeeze, and her heart skipped a beat. "I-I better go." Jo bolted from the workshop, mentally berating herself.

Of course, she was on edge because of the recent incidents. She dismissed her overreaction and spent the rest of the afternoon worrying if the sting Delta and she planned was going to blow up in their faces.

She pushed the worries aside. They didn't have much of a choice. Jo was convinced the owner of the bag of drugs was the same person who attacked Gary, attempted to break into the mercantile and destroyed her mailbox.

She was also convinced the culprit was living right under her own roof, or on the property. Raylene was off the list. All of the incidents occurred before Raylene moved in.

Which left Jo with five possible suspects...Sherry, Michelle, Julie, Leah and Kelli.

The women arrived promptly at six for dinner, and gathered around the table. Nash was right behind them. He caught Jo in the kitchen and pulled her off to the side. "Mission accomplished."

"Perfect. Thank you so much."

The dinner hour passed quickly. It was taco night, and Delta went all out with the fixings and the sides. Along with the tacos, there was Spanish rice and black beans, tortilla chips with homemade salsa and churros, a fried dough with chocolate sauce, for dessert.

Jo decided to wait until the end of the meal to announce the shed cleaning. "Since Gary is laid up, I decided to surprise him by cleaning and organizing the garden shed. I also plan to purchase a few gardening tools to surprise him."

"Do you need help?" Sherry asked.

"No. The shed is small, so I thought between Delta and me; we could knock it out first thing tomorrow morning. Thanks for the offer."

The conversation drifted to work around the farm. The women excused themselves, one by one until only Nash, Delta and Jo remained.

Jo walked Nash out onto the porch. She waited until the door closed behind them. "So the camera is ready to go?"

"Yes. My only concern is it will be dark, and we might not get a clear picture," Nash said. "I loaded the camera app on my cell phone. What time would you like me to come back to start our surveillance?"

"Maybe eight?" Jo wrinkled her nose.

"Eight it is." Nash gave Jo a thumbs up and began whistling as he sauntered across the driveway.

Delta was in the kitchen, loading the last of the dirty dishes in the dishwasher. "We ready to go?"

"As ready as we'll ever be. As soon as Nash shows up at eight, we'll get down to the business of surveilling."

*****

Nash arrived promptly at eight. They set up a small command post in Jo's office, careful to draw the blinds in case someone happened to wander past. Duke flopped down in the doorway, guarding the entrance.

It took a few minutes of fiddling with the app before Nash figured out how to project the camera onto Jo's office computer. It was a tight fit with all three of them crowding around the desk, so they decided to take turns.

The first hour passed without incident. Nash, who took the first watch, traded places with Jo. She settled in at the computer. Her mind wandered as she stared at the dark screen. Would the drugs owner show up? If it was one of the women, Jo was certain someone would show up.

But what if it wasn't one of the women? Jo quickly dismissed the thought. Of course, it was one of the women. Who else could it possibly be?

The hour passed, slowly and Jo could feel her eyelids growing heavy.

"You ready to switch?" Jo jumped at Delta's voice in her ear. She clutched her chest. "You scared me half to death."

"Sorry. I thought you heard me," Delta said. "Are you ready for me to take my turn?"

"Yes." Jo eased out of the chair. "This has to be the most boring job in the world."

Delta plunked down in the chair and set her cup of coffee on the desk. "I made some fresh coffee. Nash is beating his boredom by emptying out the leftovers in the fridge."

Jo chuckled. "Maybe I'll join him."

She found Nash at the table, devouring a chocolate chip and banana muffin. "These are good. You want a bite?"

"No thanks. I try not to eat after nine." Jo patted her hips.

"You look great," Nash lowered his eyelids, and a small smile crept across his face.

"Thanks...Nash. You look great yourself."
*Dummy!* Jo regretted her reply as soon as it was out of her mouth. "I mean, you have a great shape." Her face turned fire engine red. "You must work out."

Nash laughed. "Thank you for the compliments."

"You know what I mean."

"Yes, I do." Nash polished off the rest of the muffin and reached for his coffee. "What are the odds..."

"Hey!" Delta yelled from the office. "We got something!"

Nash bolted from his chair and ran into Jo's office, with Jo hot on his heels.

Delta began waving frantically. "I saw a flash of light. See the shadow?" she pointed excitedly.

Nash and Jo peered over her shoulder at the computer screen, still grainy and dark but with flashes of light.

"The camera caught something, but this is what I was afraid of. There's not enough light."

Jo's heart pounded loudly in her chest as the shadow moved back and forth. "Should we confront them?"

"I'll sneak around back," Nash said.

"Here, take one of my guns." Delta sprang from the chair. She ran to her room and returned with a gun case.

Nash removed the weapon. He tucked it into his waistband and strode out of the office.

Jo made sure the porch light was off before holding the back door for him. "Be careful," she whispered.

"I will." Nash disappeared into the darkness and Jo said a small prayer for his safety. She hurried back to her office. The shadow was still moving. Suddenly, the screen went black.

"Crud," Delta said. "I think they're gone."

"I hope not," Jo kept her eyes glued to the screen. There was another burst of light and motion across the screen before it went black again.

Nash returned to the office moments later. "I got there too late. They were already gone and so was the bag of marijuana."

"What a waste of time." Jo leaned against her desk, frowning at the dark screen.

"No." Delta shook her head. "Not a complete waste. We'll just move onto Plan B tomorrow morning."

# Chapter 19

Jo waited until after breakfast the next morning before tracking Nash down in his workshop. She knocked on the door and pushed it open.

Nash threw the tarp over his workbench. "What are you doing here this early?"

"I'm here for our sting, Plan B," Jo tilted her head, attempting to take a closer look at Nash's workbench. "Are you still working on your super-secret project?"

"Yes," Nash said. "It's almost done."

"I'm beginning to hate surprises," Jo joked.

"You'll like my surprise. I promise."

Deciding at the last minute Jo might need some backup for the surprise medicine cabinet inspection, Delta and Nash accompanied Jo to the women's quarters and the common area where they found most of the women waiting for their turn to shower.

Sherry did a double take. "What's going on?"

"We're having a surprise inspection," Jo said.

"A surprise inspection?" Julie shook her head.

"Yes." Jo motioned to Delta. "It looks like we're missing Raylene and Michelle."

"I'll go get them." Delta hurried out of the room.

"Tell them to bring their medicine cabinet keys."

"You're inspecting the cabinets?" Kelli asked.

"Yes. If you don't have your key with you, please go get it. We'll wait here."

Sherry and Kelli left to go get their keys. Leah pulled her key from her pocket and handed it to Jo.

Jo motioned to Julie, who was standing next to her. "Do you have your key?"

"No." Julie shook her head.

"You lost your key?"

"No. I have the key, but I'm not opening the cabinet."

"Yes, you are," Jo said. "I'm inspecting all of the cabinets."

"It's an invasion of privacy."

"You're staying on my property. Everything here belongs to me, including the contents of the cabinet."

"I won't open it." Julie crossed her arms defiantly.

"You will open it, or I'll have Nash go get the master key."

The other women returned, all silently watching the tense exchange.

Jo stared at Julie until the woman looked away.

Delta hung back near the door while Jo stepped over to the long row of medicine cabinets. One by one, the women unlocked the cabinets, and Jo inspected the contents.

Raylene was second to the last. She unlocked the cabinet door and waited for Jo to sift through the toiletries. After she finished, Jo closed the cabinet door. "Thank you, Raylene."

"You're welcome." Raylene locked the cabinet and joined the other women, who gathered off to one side.

"Julie, it's your turn."

"I already told you, this is an invasion of privacy, and I refuse to open it."

"And I told you, if you refuse to open it, I'll have Nash open it for you."

Julie's jaw clenched. "You aren't running a center to help women. You're running a detention center. This place is no better than the place we left."

"Speak for yourself," Michelle said. "Jo has done more for us than anyone, even our own families."

"Yeah," Leah agreed. "If you don't like it, you should leave."

"Ditto. Jo's our angel," Kelli chimed in.

"She saved my life," Raylene said quietly.

The room grew silent. The seconds ticked past as the standoff between Julie and Jo continued.

"Jo's gonna get in the cabinet one way or another," Delta said. "You might as well unlock it now."

"Might I point out this is grounds for removal," Jo said. "One of my rules allows random and surprise inspections."

Julie glared at Jo and then turned an angry gaze on Raylene, who was standing directly behind her. "Rules my butt. You let her in and you weren't supposed to. I guess only *you* get to break the rules."

"Master key it is." Nash stepped out of the common area as the standoff continued. He returned a short time later.

Jo pointed at Julie. "You have one final chance to unlock this cabinet or Nash opens it."

"Fine. I'll unlock the cabinet." Julie marched across the room. "I wouldn't put it past you to plant something inside."

Julie reached into her pocket and pulled out a key. She unlocked the padlock and stepped aside. "Have at it."

Jo placed the lock on top of the cabinet and opened the door. Julie's toothbrush and toothpaste were on the bottom shelf, along with a small box of Band-Aids and hand lotion.

The next shelf contained body wash, shampoo and conditioner. Dental floss, a small disposable razor and a pair of tweezers were on the top shelf.

"See? You wasted your time," Julie snarled. "This was nothing but a witch hunt."

Jo ignored the woman's rant, searching the cabinet one last time. She stopped when she got to the box of Band-Aids. She slowly pulled the box off the shelf and gave it a quick shake.

She flipped the flap and peered inside. "What is this?" Jo carefully removed the familiar Ziploc bag filled with pot along with a wad of cash. She set the bag on the table and slowly counted the money. "How much money was missing from the cash register yesterday, Raylene?"

"Fifty-dollars."

"Fifty-dollars." Jo counted out a twenty-dollar bill, a ten-dollar bill and twenty ones. "Fifty-dollars, Julie."

"So I set some money aside, so what?"

Jo dropped the cash on the table and picked up the bag of drugs. She opened the bag and took a whiff. "This is marijuana."

"It's a plant!" Julie screamed. "You set me up." She spun on her heel and took a step toward Raylene. "This is a frame job. You set me up, just so you could keep your little pet project, Raylene here, and get rid of me, even after you found a weapon in her room."

"What weapon in Raylene's room?" Jo forced her voice to remain calm.

"Th-the multi-tool," Julie stammered. "The one you found in her room."

"You planted that in my room." Raylene took a menacing step toward Julie. "You're the one who set me up!"

Nash, certain the situation was getting out of control, stepped between the women.

No one noticed that Delta slipped out earlier and returned just in time for the fireworks.

"I think I've heard enough." Jo waved the bag of marijuana. "You were smoking pot in the garden shed. When Gary almost busted you, and you realized he suspected something was up, you attacked him. You set Raylene up by stealing money from the cash register, claiming it was her who took the money."

"Possession of drugs is grounds for immediate removal. You can take all of the belongings from your room. They're yours to keep." She handed Julie the fifty dollars. "While you pack, I'll purchase your bus ticket to Kansas City, and Nash and I will drive you to the nearest bus station."

"You can't kick me out." Julie jabbed her finger in Raylene's shoulder. "What about her?"

It was the last straw. Raylene flung both arms around Julie, catching her off balance and knocking her to the floor.

"Get off me," Julie writhed wildly, trying to escape Raylene's ironclad grip.

"Everyone step back." Deputy Brian Franklin rushed into the room, his gun drawn.

Raylene released her grip and rolled to the side.

Julie flipped onto her knees and scrambled to her feet. "This woman attacked me!"

"She did not," Nash said.

"You saw it!" Julie shouted. "You all saw it!"

"Julie started it," Leah said. "She jabbed Raylene and Raylene defended herself."

The officer lifted his radio. "I need some backup. I've got a domestic dispute over at 712 D Road in Divine."

"Backup is on the way."

"We can do this the easy way, or we can do it the hard way." The deputy put a light hand on Julie's arm.

She jerked away. "Don't touch me."

"Hard way it is." The deputy unclipped his handcuffs and snapped one on Julie's wrist. "You have the right to remain silent."

Julie struggled to get away.

Nash raced across the room to help.

All the while Julie screamed obscenities at them, most of them aimed at Jo and Raylene.

She continued to scream until the deputy led her out of the building.

Jo waited until it was quiet and Julie was gone. "I'm sorry you all had to witness this."

"Don't apologize, Jo. You did what you had to do." Sherry patted Jo's arm. "I want you to know how much I appreciate all you've done for me."

"Me, too." Michelle slipped in next to Sherry.

"We all do," Kelli chimed in. "Please don't think badly of the rest of us."

"Of course I don't."

"You gave her a second chance, and she took advantage of you," Nash said. "It happens to the best of us."

"Thank you, Nash." Jo caught Delta's eye. "Thank you Delta, for thinking ahead and calling the police."

"Jo, if I could have a word with you." The deputy stepped back inside. "I have a few loose ends to wrap up."

"We'll get back to work." The women quietly exited the building, leaving Jo, Delta, Nash and Raylene behind.

Jo briefly explained all that transpired and her belief Julie was responsible for not only the vandalism but also Gary's attack.

"Would you like to press charges for today's incident and her assault on Raylene?"

Jo clasped her hands. "I...I don't...."

"Jo..." Delta warned.

"But I will." Jo handed the deputy the bag of drugs. "This also belongs to Julie. What will the courts do to her?"

"She's on probation," the deputy said. "Chances are she'll return to prison."

"That's what I thought."

Delta could see Jo was having second thoughts.

"You must do the right thing," Delta said. "Otherwise, there may be even more victims down the road. Think of Gary."

"We have no proof she was the one who struck him," Jo said.

"I sent the hoe to the lab for fingerprinting," Deputy Franklin said. "Now that we have a suspect, we'll see if we have a match between Ms. Canner's fingerprints and those found on the hoe. She insists you're running a second rate prison and she wants to file a complaint."

"Seriously?" Jo shuddered. "Where did so much hate come from?"

"I don't know, but from the way she's going on, it's a good thing she's out of here. I think you were headed for even more trouble."

The deputy finished taking notes, secured the bag of marijuana in an evidence bag and promised to contact Jo later.

Jo and the others accompanied the deputy to his car, which was parked next to a second patrol car.

Jo could see Julie in the back seat, but she never turned to look at them.

"She is a troubled woman," Delta said. "Hopefully, she'll be gone for a very long time."

# Chapter 20

"Delta, are you giving Duke table scraps again?" Jo scolded.

"Who me?" Delta asked innocently.

Jo cleared her throat.

"Fine. But it was only a small sliver of meat, and I can't stand how he looks at me with those sad eyes."

"He does that to all of us," Michelle laughed.

"Duke is working his way around the table," Sherry said

The dog padded over to Jo with the same pitiful look on his face.

"You're busted, buddy."

Duke sniffed Jo's hand and trotted off to his bed in the corner.

Gary was finally on the mend and decided to join them for dinner. "I talked to Sheriff Franklin before I came down here. Julie's fingerprints matched the prints on the hoe. Because of the link to my attack, she went before the judge today. She violated her probation and is on her way back to the *Central State Women's Penitentiary* to finish serving her sentence."

"Such a shame," Jo shook her head. "I had no idea she was behind your attack."

"The sheriff said she confessed to trying to break into the mercantile," Gary said.

"But why? Why risk an opportunity for a second chance?"

"I don't know. Could be the drugs," Gary said. "They're sending her in for a psychiatric evaluation."

"I'm glad she was caught," Delta said.

"Me, too," Nash said. "Now that dinner is over, the ladies and I have a surprise for you, Jo."

"Is this the super-secret project you've been working on for weeks now?" Jo teased.

"It is." Nash grinned.

"We can't wait for you to see it." Sherry clapped her hands.

"Nash made sure we all had a hand in helping," Raylene said.

"Even me," Delta laughed.

"I can't wait to see it," Jo said.

Nash slipped out of his chair and strode out of the room. The back door slammed and he returned moments later carrying a large wrapped package. "This is a small token of our appreciation for all that you've done. We want you to know how special you are, Jo."

"You've done so much for everyone around you," Gary said quietly. "Even me, a lonely old farmer."

"And us," Michelle motioned to the other women. "You're our own angel. You've given us hope."

"And a second chance," Leah said.

Jo's throat swelled and tears burned the back of her eyes. "I...don't know what to say."

"Go ahead, open it," Sherry said.

Jo slid out of her chair and joined Nash. "It's almost too pretty to unwrap. Let me take a picture." She darted up the stairs and returned with camera in hand. "All of you gather around the package."

There was a collective groan, but no one argued as they all gathered next to Nash while Jo snapped several pictures.

"Now open it," Delta said.

Jo set her camera on the table and gingerly removed the brightly colored wrapping paper. Inside was a wooden sign, anchored to an oval wrought iron frame.

"It's a sign." Jo finished ripping the paper off and took a step back. "Divine Farms. Est. 2019."

"It's a sign for the yard," Nash explained. "I already put the post up out front."

"You put in a post?" Jo followed Nash onto the porch. The others followed behind.

"Well, I'll be. I never even noticed it."

"I did it before dinner. The cement has already set, so I think it's safe to add the sign."

The women and Gary watched as Nash screwed the sign to the post.

Jo pressed a hand to her chest, tears streaming down her cheeks at the sign made especially for her. "Divine Farms," she breathed. "It has a nice ring to it."

She hugged each of them as she thanked them for the priceless gift. In turn, they thanked Jo for giving them a second chance.

Jo proudly stood in front of the sign as Nash and the others snapped pictures.

One by one, they straggled back inside, but Jo hung back, staring at the sign and reflecting on how her life had changed over the last year.

She didn't notice Delta had returned. "You're a good woman, Joanna Pepperdine."

"Thank you, Delta." Jo swiped at her wet face. "And you're a wonderful friend. Thank you for joining me on this journey."

"I wouldn't have it any other way." Delta slipped her arm through Jo's arm. "Now what are we going to do about Raylene?"

The end.

*If you enjoyed reading "Divine Intervention," please take a moment to leave a review. It would mean so much to me. Thank you! Hope Callaghan*

**The series continues...Book 2 in the "Divine Cozy Mystery Series" coming soon!**

# Get Free eBooks and More

Sign up for my Free Cozy Mysteries Newsletter to get free and discounted ebooks, giveaways & soon-to-be-released books!

**hopecallaghan.com/newsletter**

# List of Hope Callaghan Books

*Get The eBook Version FREE*

*When You Buy The Paperback*

## Divine Cozy Mystery Series

Divine Intervention: Book 1

Divine Secrets: Book 2 (Coming Soon!)

Divine Cozy Mystery Book 3 (Coming Soon!)

## Made in Savannah Cozy Mystery Series

Key to Savannah: Book 1
Road to Savannah: Book 2
Justice in Savannah: Book 3
Swag in Savannah: Book 4
Trouble in Savannah: Book 5
Missing in Savannah: Book 6
Setup in Savannah: Book 7
Merry Masquerade: Book 8
The Family Affair: Book 9
Pirates in Peril: Book 10

Matrimony & Mayhem: Book 11
Book 12: Coming Soon!
**Made in Savannah Box Set I (Books 1-3)**

### *Garden Girls Cozy Mystery Series*

Who Murdered Mr. Malone? Book 1
Grandkids Gone Wild: Book 2
Smoky Mountain Mystery: Book 3
Death by Dumplings: Book 4
Eye Spy: Book 5
Magnolia Mansion Mysteries: Book 6
Missing Milt: Book 7
Bully in the 'Burbs: Book 8
Fall Girl: Book 9
Home for the Holidays: Book 10
Sun, Sand, and Suspects: Book 11
Look Into My Ice: Book 12
Forget Me Knot: Book 13
Nightmare in Nantucket: Book 14
Greed with Envy: Book 15
Dying for Dollars: Book 16
Stranger Among Us: Book 17
Dash For Cash: Book 18
Arsonist and Lace: Book 19
Court of Corruption: Book 20
Framed in Florida: Book 21
Book 22: Coming Soon!
Garden Girls Box Set I – (Books 1-3)
Garden Girls Box Set II – (Books 4-6)
Garden Girls Box Set III – (Books 7-9)

## *Cruise Ship Cozy Mystery Series*

Starboard Secrets: Book 1
Portside Peril: Book 2
Lethal Lobster:  Book 3
Deadly Deception: Book 4
Vanishing Vacationers: Book 5
Cruise Control: Book 6
Killer Karaoke: Book 7
Suite Revenge: Book 8
Cruisin' for a Bruisin': Book 9
High Seas Heist: Book 10
Family, Friends and Foes: Book 11
Murder on Main: Book 12
Fatal Flirtation: Book 13
Deadly Delivery: Book 14
Reindeer & Robberies: Book 15
Book 16: Coming Soon!
Cruise Ship Cozy Mysteries Box Set I (Books 1-3)
Cruise Ship Cozy Mysteries Box Set II (Books 4-6)
Cruise Ship Cozy Mysteries Box Set III (Books 7-9)

## *Sweet Southern Sleuths Cozy Mysteries*
## *Short Stories Series*

Teepees and Trailer Parks: Book 1
Bag of Bones: Book 2

Southern Stalker: Book 3
Two Settle the Score: Book 4
Killer Road Trip: Book 5
Pups in Peril: Book 6
Dying To Get Married-In: Book 7
Deadly Drive-In: Book 8
Secrets of a Stranger: Book 9
Library Lockdown: Book 10
Vandals & Vigilantes: Book 11
Fatal Frolic: Book 12
Sweet Southern Sleuths Box Set I: (Books 1-4)
Sweet Southern Sleuths Box Set: II: (Books 5-8)
Sweet Southern Sleuths Box Set III: (Books 9-12)
Sweet Southern Sleuths 12 Book Box Set (Entire Series)

### *Samantha Rite Deception Mystery Series*

Waves of Deception: Book 1

Winds of Deception: Book 2

Tides of Deception: Book 3

Samantha Rite Series Box Set

(Books 1-3-The Complete Series)

## Cozy Mystery Collections

Hope Callaghan Cozy Mysteries: 6 Book Collection (Fall & Family Edition)

Cozy Mysteries 12 Book Box Set: (Garden Girls & Cruise Ship Cozy Mystery Series)

Hope Callaghan Cozy Mysteries: 6 Book Collection (Home & Holiday Edition)

Hope Callaghan Cozy Mysteries: 4 Book Collection (1st in Series Edition)

## Audiobooks
## (On Sale Now or FREE with Audible Trial)

Key to Savannah: Book 1 (Made in Savannah Series)

Road to Savannah: Book 2 (Made in Savannah Series)

Justice in Savannah: Book 3 (Made in Savannah Series)

## Cozy Mysteries Cookbook (FREE)

Cozy Mysteries Cookbook-Recipes From Hope Callaghan Books

# Meet the Author

Hope loves to connect with her readers! Connect with her today!

**Never miss another book deal! Text the word Books to 33222**

Visit **hopecallaghan.com/newsletter** for special offers, free books, and soon-to-be-released books!

**Pinterest:**
https://www.pinterest.com/cozymysteriesauthor/

**Facebook:**
https://www.facebook.com/authorhopecallaghan/

**Instagram:**
https://www.instagram.com/hopecallaghanauthor/

Hope Callaghan is an American author who loves to write Christian books, especially Christian Mystery and Cozy Mystery books. She has written more than 50 mystery books (and counting) in six series.

In March 2017, Hope won a Mom's Choice Award for her book, "Key to Savannah," Book 1 in the Made in Savannah Cozy Mystery Series.

Born and raised in a small town in West Michigan, she now lives in Florida with her husband.

She is the proud mother of one daughter and a stepdaughter and stepson. When she's not doing the thing she loves best - writing books - she enjoys cooking, traveling and reading books.

# Chocolate Chip, Banana Nut Muffins Recipe

<u>Ingredients</u>:

1 tbsp. instant coffee granules

1 tbsp. hot water

3 bananas, mashed

1 cup butter, softened

1-1/4 cups sugar

1 egg

2-1/2 cups flour

1 tsp. baking powder

½ tsp. baking soda

½ tsp. salt

1 cup semi-sweet chocolate chips

½ cup chopped walnuts

## Directions:

-Preheat oven to 350 degrees.

-Dissolve coffee in hot water.

-Stir in mashed bananas.

-Cream together butter, egg and sugar.

-Add to banana mixture.

-Sift together flour, baking soda, baking powder and salt.

-Stir dry mixture into creamed mixture.

-Fold in chocolate chips and walnuts.

-Line muffin tins or grease muffin tins.

-Bake at 350 degrees for 18-20 minutes.

*Recipe is for 12 large muffins. If making smaller muffins, adjust baking time. Remove from oven when toothpick comes out clean.

CPSIA information can be obtained
at www.ICGtesting.com
Printed in the USA
BVHW031313180421
605248BV00013B/960

9 781793 941558